MONSTER HIGH

Also by
LISI HARRISON

Alphas
Alphas
Movers and Fakers

The Clique
The Clique
Best Friends for Never
Revenge of the Wannabes
Invasion of the Boy Snatchers
The Pretty Committee Strikes Back
Dial L for Loser
It's Not Easy Being Mean
Sealed with a Diss
Bratfest at Tiffany's
The Clique Summer Collection
P.S. I Loathe You
Boys R Us
Charmed and Dangerous: The Rise of the Pretty Committee
The Cliquetionary
These Boots Are Made for Stalking
My Little Phony

A novel by
Lisi Harrison

poppy

LITTLE, BROWN AND COMPANY
New York Boston

Poppy

Hachette Book Group
237 Park Avenue, New York, NY 10017
For more of your favorite series, visit our website at www.pickapoppy.com

Poppy is an imprint of Little, Brown and Company.
The Poppy name and logo are trademarks of Hachette Book Group, Inc.

First Edition: September 2010

Library of Congress Cataloging-in-Publication Data
Harrison, Lisi.
    Monster high : a novel / by Lisi Harrison.—1st ed.
        p. cm.
    "Poppy."
    Summary: Frankie Stein was created in a laboratory, and when she enters Merston High School camouflaged as a "normie," all she wants is to fit in, but it takes the help of another new student who believes that everyone should be treated equally before Frankie even has a chance.
    ISBN 978-0-316-09918-9
    [1. Prejudices—Fiction. 2. Monsters—Fiction. 3. Cliques (Sociology)—Fiction. 4. High schools—Fiction. 5. Schools—Fiction. 6. Oregon—Fiction.] I. Title.
    PZ7.H2527Mo 2010
    [Fic]—dc22

10 9 8 7 6 5 4 3

RRD-C

Printed in the United States of America

For Richard Abate: my loyal friend, brilliant agent, fellow gum-chomper, and tireless brainstormer. Thank you times a billion. F.U.P.M.

CONTENTS

PROLOGUE

Frankie Stein's thick lashes fluttered open. Flashes of bright white light strobed before her as she strained to focus, but her eyelids were too heavy to lift all the way. The room went dark.

"Her cerebral cortex has been loaded," announced a man, his deep voice a blend of satisfaction and fatigue.

"Can she hear us?" asked a woman.

"Hear, see, understand, and identify more than four hundred objects," he replied, delighted. "If I continue filling her brain with information, in two weeks she'll have the intelligence and physical capabilities of a typical fifteen-year-old." He paused. "Okay, maybe a little smarter than that. But she'll be fifteen."

"Oh, Viktor, this is the happiest moment of my life." The woman sniffled. "She's perfect."

"I know." He sniffed too. "Daddy's perfect little girl."

They took turns kissing Frankie's forehead. One of them smelled like chemicals, the other like sweet flowers. Together, they smelled like love.

Frankie tried to open her eyes again. This time she could barely make them flutter.

"She blinked!" the woman exclaimed. "She's trying to look at us! Frankie, I'm Viveka, your mommy. Can you see me?"

"She can't," Viktor said.

Frankie's body tensed at the sound of those words. How could someone else decide what she was capable of? It didn't make sense.

"Why not?" her mother seemed to ask for both of them.

"Her battery pack is almost drained. She needs a charge."

"So charge her!"

Yeah, charge me! Charge me! Charge me!

More than anything, Frankie wanted to see these four hundred objects. Wanted to study her parents' faces while they identified each object in their kind voices. Wanted to come to life and explore the world she had just been born into. But she couldn't move.

"I can't charge her until her bolts finish setting," her father explained.

Viveka started to cry, her gentle sobs no longer sounding joyful.

"It's okay, sweetie," Viktor cooed. "A few more hours and she'll be completely stable."

"It's not that." Viveka inhaled sharply.

"Then what?"

"She's so beautiful and full of potential, and it..." She sniffed again. "It just breaks my heart that she'll have to live...you know...like us."

"What's wrong with *us*?" he asked. Yet something in his voice suggested that he already knew.

She snickered. "You're kidding, right?"

"Viv, things won't be like this forever," Viktor said. "Times will change. You'll see."

"How? Who's going to change them?"

"I don't know. Someone will…eventually."

"Well, I hope we're around to see it," she said, sighing.

"We will be," Viktor assured her. "We Steins tend to live long lives."

Viveka giggled softly.

Frankie desperately wanted to know what about these "times" needed to "change." But asking became unimaginable as her battery drained completely. Feeling both light-headed and impossibly heavy at the same time, Frankie floated deeper into the darkness, settling in a place where she could no longer hear the people around her. She could not recall their conversation or smell their flower- and chemical-scented necks.

All Frankie could do was hope that by the time she woke up, that *thing* Viveka wanted to be "around to see" would be there. And if it wasn't, that Frankie herself would have the strength to get it for her.

CHAPTER ONE
NEWFOUND FABULOUSNESS

The fourteen-hour drive from Beverly Hills, California, to Salem, Oregon, had been total Gitmo. It went from road trip to guilt trip in less than a minute. And the torture didn't let up for nine hundred miles. Faking sleep was Melody Carver's only escape.

"Welcome to *bOre*-egon," her older sister mumbled as they crossed the state line. "Or should I call it *snOre*-egon? How about *abhOre*-egon? Or maybe—"

"That's enough, Candace!" her father snapped from the driver's seat of their new BMW diesel SUV. Green in both color and fuel efficiency, it was one of the many overtures her parents had taken to show the locals that Beau and Glory Carver were more than just great-looking wealthy transplants from the 90210.

The thirty-six preshipped UPS boxes filled with kayaks, sailboards, fishing poles, canteens, instructional wine-tasting DVDs, organic trail mix, camping gear, bear traps, walkie-talkies, crampons, ice picks, cobra hammers, adzes, skis, boots, poles, snowboards, helmets, Burton outerwear, and flannel underwear were just a few more.

But Candace's comments became even louder when it started to rain. "Ahhhhhh, August in *pOre*-egon!" Candace sniffed. "Ain't it grand?" An eye roll followed. Melody didn't have to see it to know. Still, she peeked out through barely opened lids to confirm.

"Ugggggh!" Candace kicked the back of her mother's seat indignantly. Then she blew her nose and whipped the moist tissue at Melody's shoulder. Melody's heart beat faster, but she managed to hold still. It was easier than fighting back.

"I don't get it," Candace continued. "Melody survived fifteen years breathing smog. One more won't kill her. She could wear a mask. People could sign it, like they sign casts. Maybe it would inspire a whole line of accessories for asthmatics. Like inhalers on necklaces and—"

"Enough, Candi." Glory sighed, obviously exhausted from the monthlong debate.

"But next September I'll be in college," Candace pressed, not used to losing an argument. She was blond, perfectly proportioned, and used to getting what she wanted. "You couldn't wait one more year to move?"

"This move will be good for all of us. It's not just about your sister's asthma. Merston High is one of Oregon's top schools. Plus, it's about connecting with nature and getting away from all that Beverly Hills superficiality."

Melody smiled to herself. Her father, Beau, was a celebrated plastic surgeon, and her mother had been a personal shopper to the stars. Superficiality was their master. They were its zombies. Still, Melody appreciated her mother's ongoing effort to keep

Candace from blaming her for the move. Even though it kind of *was* her fault.

In a family of genetically perfect human beings, Melody Carver was an anomaly. A rarity. An oddity. Abnormal.

Beau had been blessed with Italian good looks despite his SoCal roots. The flicker in his black eyes was like sunshine on a lake. His smile warmed like cashmere, and his perma-tan had done zero damage to his forty-six-year-old skin. With just the right stubble-to-hair-gel ratio, he had as many male patients as female ones. Each one hoped to peel off the bandages and look ageless... just like Beau.

Glory was forty-two but, thanks to her husband, her blemish-free skin had been nipped and tucked long before she needed the procedures. She seemed to have one pedicured foot off the human development chart and into the next stage of evolution—a stage that defied gravity and ceased to age her past thirty-four. With wavy shoulder-length auburn hair, aqua blue eyes, and lips so naturally puffed they needed no collagen, Glory could have modeled had she not been so petite. Everyone said so. At any rate, she swore personal shopping always would have been her career choice, *even if* Beau had given her calf extensions.

Lucky Candace was a combination of both her parents. Like an alpha predator, she had filled up on the good stuff, leaving scraps for the next offspring in line. While the petite frame she inherited from her mother hurt her potential modeling career, it did wonders for her wardrobe, which was bursting with hand-me-downs that included everything from Gap to Gucci (but mostly Gucci). She had Glory's blue-green eyes and Beau's sunny sparkle, Beau's tan and Glory's airbrushed complexion. Her cheekbones ascended like marble banisters. And her long hair, which happily assumed the texture of straight or wavy, was the color of butter drizzled with melted toffee. Candi's friends (and their mothers) would snap photos of her square jaw, strong chin, or straight nose and give them to Beau with the hopes that his hands could work the same miracles his DNA once did. And, of course, they did.

Even with Melody.

Convinced the wrong family had taken her home from the hospital, Melody placed little value on physical appearance. What was the point? Her chin was scant, her teeth were fanglike, and her hair was a flat black. No highlights. No lowlights. No butter or toffee drizzle. Just flat black. Her eyes, while fully functional, were as steel gray and narrow as a skeptical cat's. Not that anyone noticed her eyes. Her nose took center stage. Composed of two bumps and a sharp drop-off, it looked like a camel in downward-facing dog.

Not that it mattered. As far as Melody was concerned, the ability to sing was her best asset. Music teachers had gushed over her pitch-perfect voice. Clear, angelic, and haunting, it had a mesmerizing effect on everyone who heard it, and teary audiences would spring to their feet after every recital. Unfortunately, by the time she turned eight, asthma had taken center stage and stolen the show.

Once Melody started middle school, Beau offered to operate. But Melody refused. A new nose wouldn't cure her asthma, so why bother? All she had to do was hold out until high school, and things would change. Girls would be less superficial. Boys would be more mature. And academia would reign supreme.

Ha!

Things got worse when Melody started at Beverly Hills High. Girls called her Smellody because of her giant nose—and boys didn't call her anything at all. They didn't even look at her. By Thanksgiving she was practically invisible. If it weren't for her incessant wheezing and inhaler sucking, no one would have known she was alive.

Beau couldn't stand to see his daughter—who was "full of symmetric potential"—suffer any further. That Christmas, he told Melody that Santa got a new form of rhinoplasty approved, promising to open up airways and alleviate asthma. Maybe she'd be able to sing again.

"How wonderful!" Glory placed her small hands together in prayer and then lifted her eyes toward the skylight in gratitude.

"No more Rudolph the big-nosed reindeer," Candace joked.

"This is about her health, not her looks, Candace," scolded Beau, obviously trying to meet Melody halfway.

"Wow! Amazing." Melody hugged her father in thanks, even though she wasn't sure noses had anything to do with restricted bronchi. But pretending to believe his explanation gave her *some* hope. And it was easier than admitting that her family was embarrassed by her face.

Over Christmas break, Melody underwent the surgery. She woke up to find she had a thin, pert Jessica Biel nose, and dental veneers instead of almost-fangs. By the end of the recovery period, she had lost five pounds and gained access to her mother's Gap to Gucci (but mostly Gucci) hand-me-downs. Unfortunately, she still couldn't sing.

Back at Beverly Hills High, the girls were welcoming, the boys were gawking, and hummingbirds seemed to fly a little closer. She found a level of acceptance she had never dreamed possible.

But none of this newfound fabulousness made Melody any

happier. Instead of flaunting and flirting, she spent her free time buried under the covers feeling like her sister's metallic Tory Burch tote—beautiful and shiny on the surface but a terrible mess on the inside. *How dare they act nice just because I'm pretty! I'm the same person I've always been!*

By summer, Melody had completely withdrawn. She dressed in baggy clothes, never brushed her hair, and accessorized solely by clipping an inhaler to her belt loops.

During the Carvers' annual Fourth of July barbecue (where she used to sing the national anthem), Melody had a severe asthma attack that landed her in Cedars-Sinai Medical Center. In the waiting room, Glory anxiously flipped through a travel magazine and stopped at a lush photograph of Oregon, claiming she could smell the fresh air just by looking at it. When Melody was released, her parents told her they were moving. And for the first time ever, a smile spread across her perfectly symmetrical face.

"*Helloooooo, adOre-egon!*" she said to herself as the green BMW forged ahead.

Then, lulled by the rhythmic swish of the windshield wipers and the tapping of falling rain, Melody drifted off to sleep.

This time for real.

CHAPTER TWO
LIFE'S A STITCH

The sun was finally up. Robins and sparrows were chirping their usual morning playlists. Outside Frankie's frosted bedroom window, kids on bikes began ringing their bells and circling the Radcliffe Way cul-de-sac. The neighborhood was awake. She could finally blast Lady Gaga.

"I can see myself in the movies, with my picture in the city lights..."

More than anything, Frankie wanted to bop her head to "The Fame." No. Wait. That wasn't entirely true. What she *really* wanted to do was jump up on her metal bed, kick the fleece-coated electromagnetic blankets to the polished concrete, swing her hair, wave her arms, shake her booty, *and* bop her head to "The Fame." But disrupting the flow of electricity before the charge was complete could lead to memory loss, fainting spells, or even a coma. The plus side, however, was never needing to plug in her iPod touch. As long as it was near Frankie's body, the device's battery had more juice than Tropicana.

Luxuriating in her morning infusion, she lay supine with a tangle of black and red wires clamped to her neck bolts. While the last electric currents ricocheted through Frankie's body, she leafed through the latest issue of *Seventeen* magazine. Careful not to smudge her hardening In the Navy nail polish, she searched the models' smooth, odd-colored necks for metal rivets, wondering how they managed to "amp" without them.

As soon as Carmen Electra (the name she'd given the amp machine, because its technical name was too hard to pronounce) shut down, Frankie delighted in the itchy tingle of her thimble-size neck bolts when they started to cool. Feeling invigorated, she pressed her pert nose into the magazine and took a long sniff of the enclosed Miss Dior Cherie perfume sample.

"You like?" she asked, waving it in front of the Glitterati. Five white rats stood on their pink hind feet and scratched the glass wall of their cage. A flurry of nontoxic multicolored glitter slid off their backs like snow from an awning.

Frankie took one more sniff. "Me too." She waved the folded paper through the cold formaldehyde-laced air and got up to light her vanilla-scented candles. The vinegary chemical odor of the solution was seeping into her hair and dominating the floral notes in her Pantene conditioner.

"Do I smell vanilla?" her dad asked as he rapped on the closed door.

Frankie shut off her music. "Yesssss!" she trilled, ignoring his pretending-to-be-annoyed tone—a tone he'd been using since Frankie transformed his lab into a "Fab." She heard it when she glammed up the laboratory rats, began storing lip gloss and hair accessories in his beakers, and glued Justin Bieber's face to the skeleton (*because, how voltage is that poster where he's sitting on the skateboard?*). But she knows her dad didn't really mind. It was her bedroom now too. And besides, if he really cared, he wouldn't refer to her as—

"How is Daddy's perfect little girl?" Viktor Stein knocked again and then opened the door. Frankie's mother followed Viktor into the room.

Viktor was swinging a leather duffel and wearing a black Adidas tracksuit and his favorite brown UGG slippers with a hole in one toe.

"Worn and old, just like Viv," he'd say when Frankie made fun of them, and then his wife would swat him on the arm. But Frankie knew he was just joking, because Viveka was the type of woman you wished was in a magazine just so you could stare at her violet-colored eyes and shiny black hair without being called a stalker or a freak.

Her father, however, had more of an Arnold Schwarzenegger thing going on, as if his chiseled features had been stretched to cover his square head. People probably wanted to stare at him too but were afraid of his six-foot-four frame and super-squinty expression. But his squints didn't mean he was angry. They meant he was thinking. And being a mad scientist, he was always thinking. . . . At least that's how Viveka explained it.

"Can we talk to you for a minute, sweetie?" Viveka asked in a singsong way that mimicked the swooshing hem of her black crepe sundress. Her voice was so delicate that people were shocked when they heard it coming from a six-foot-tall woman.

Viv and Vik walked across the polished concrete floor holding hands, a united front, as always. But this time, traces of concern lay beneath their proud grins.

"Have a seat, dear." Viveka gestured to the pillow-covered ruby-red Moroccan chaise Frankie had ordered online from Ikea. In the far corner of the Fab, along with her sticker-covered desk, her flat-screen Sony, and a rainbow of colorful wardrobes stuffed with Internet buys, the lounge faced the only window in the room. Even though that window had been frosted for privacy, it gave Frankie a glimpse into the real world—or at least the promise of one.

Frankie padded across the fluffy pink sheepskin path from her bed to the lounge, silently fearing that her parents had seen her latest charges from iTunes. Nervous, she pulled on the track of fine black stitches that held her head in place.

"Don't pull," Viktor insisted, lowering himself onto the chaise. The birch frame creaked in protest. "There's nothing to be nervous about. We just want to talk to you." He placed the leather duffel by his feet.

Viveka tapped the empty cushion beside her, then fussed with her signature black muslin scarf. But Frankie, fearing a lecture on the value of a dollar, tightened her silky black Harajuku Lovers robe and chose to sit on the pink rug instead.

"What's up?" she asked, smiling and trying to sound as if she hadn't just spent $59.99 for a season pass of *Gossip Girl*.

"Change is in the air." Viktor rubbed his hands together and inhaled deeply, as if gearing up to tackle a hike up Mount Hood.

No more credit cards? Frankie speculated with dread.

Viveka nodded and forced another smile, her dark purple painted lips holding tight to each other. She looked at her husband, urging him to continue, but he widened his dark eyes to communicate that he didn't know what to say

Frankie shifted uncomfortably on the rug. She had never seen her parents at such a loss for words. She fast-forwarded through her recent purchases, hoping to figure out which item had tipped them over the edge. *Season pass of* Gossip Girl—*orange blossom room spray—striped Hot Sox with the cute toe holes—magazine subscriptions for* Us Weekly, Seventeen, Teen Vogue, Cosmo-Girl—*horoscope app—numerology app—dream interpreter app—Morrocanoil hair de-frizzer—Current/Elliott boyfriend jeans...*

Nothing too major. Still, the anticipation was making her neck bolts spark.

"Relax, dear." Viveka leaned forward and smoothed her hand over Frankie's long black hair. The soothing gesture stopped the energy leak but did nothing for her insides. They were still popping and hissing like the Fourth of July. Her parents were the only people Frankie knew. They were her best friends and mentors. Disappointing them meant disappointing the entire world.

Viktor took another deep breath, then exhaled as he made his announcement. "The summer is over. Your mother and I have to go back to teaching science and anatomy at the university. We can't home school you anymore." He jiggled his ankle restlessly.

"Huh?" Frankie knit her perfectly sculpted eyebrows. *What can this possibly have to do with shopping?*

Viveka placed an *I'll-take-it-from-here* hand on Viktor's knee, then cleared her throat. "What your father is trying to say is that you are fifteen days old. On each of those days, he implanted a year's worth of knowledge into your brain: math, science, history, geography, languages, technology, art, music, movies, songs, trends, expressions, social conventions, manners, emotional depth, maturity, discipline, free will, muscle coordination, speech coordination, sense recognition, depth perception, ambition, and even a small appetite. You have it all!"

Frankie nodded her head, wondering when the shopping part was coming.

"So, now that you're a beautiful, smart teenage girl, you're ready for..." Viveka sniffed back a tear. She looked over at Viktor, who nodded, urging her to continue. Licking her lips and exhaling, she managed to work up one last smile, then—

Frankie sparked. This was taking longer than ground shipping.

Finally Viveka blurted, "Normie school." She said it like *nor-mee.*

"What's 'normie'?" Frankie asked, fearing the answer. *Is that some kind of rehab program for shopoholics?*

"A normie is someone with common physical traits," Viktor explained.

"Like..." Viveka picked up an issue of *Teen Vogue* from the orange-lacquered side table and opened it to a random page. "Like them."

She tapped an H&M ad featuring three girls in bras and hot pants—a blond, a brunette, and a redhead. They all had curly hair.

"Am I a normie?" Frankie asked, feeling just as proud as the beaming models.

Viveka shook her head from side to side.

"Why? Because my hair is straight?" Frankie asked. This was the most confusing lesson of all.

"No, not because your hair is straight," Viktor said through a frustrated smirk. "Because I built you."

"Didn't everyone's parents 'build' them?" Frankie made air quotes. "You know, technically speaking."

Viveka raised a dark eyebrow. Her daughter had a point.

"Yes, but I built you in the literal way," Viktor explained. "In this lab. From perfect body parts that I made with my hands. I programmed your brain full of information, stitched you together, and put bolts on the sides of your neck so you could get charged. You have no real need for food, other than enjoyment. And, Frankie, because you have no blood, well, your skin, it's…it's *green*."

Frankie looked at her hands as if for the first time. They were the color of mint chocolate chip ice cream, just like the rest of her.

"I know," she giggled. "Isn't it voltage?"

"It *is*." Viktor chuckled. "That's why you're so special. No other student at your new school was made like that. Just you."

"You mean the school will have other people in it?" Frankie looked around the Fab, the only room she'd ever truly known.

Viktor and Viveka nodded, guilt and trepidation wrinkling their foreheads.

Frankie searched their moist eyes, wondering if this was really happening. Were they really going to just cut her loose? Drop her in a school full of curly-haired normies and expect her to fend for herself? Did they really have the heart to walk away from her education so they could teach lecture halls full of perfect strangers instead?

Despite their quivering lips and salt-stained cheeks, it seemed that they actually were. Suddenly, a feeling that could only be measured on the Richter scale rumbled through Frankie's belly. It climbed up her chest, shot through her throat, and exploded right out of her mouth:

"VOLTAGE!"

CHAPTER THREE
YOU'VE GOT MALE

"We're here!" Beau announced, beeping his horn repeatedly. "Wakey, wakey!"

Melody peeled her ear off the cool window and opened her eyes. At first glance, the neighborhood seemed to be covered in cotton. But her vision sharpened like a developing Polaroid as her eyes adjusted to the hazy morning light.

The two moving trucks blocked access to their circular driveway and obstructed the view of the house. All Melody could make out was half of a wraparound porch and its requisite swing, both of which appeared to be made of life-size Lincoln Logs. It was an image Melody would never forget. Or was it the emotions the image conjured—hope, excitement, and fear of the unknown, all three tightly braided together, creating a fourth emotion that was impossible to define. She was getting a second chance at happiness, and it tickled like swallowing fifty fuzzy caterpillars.

Beepbeepbeepbeep!

A husky mountain man wearing baggy jeans and a brown puffy Carhartt vest nodded hello as he pulled the Carvers' eggplant-colored Calvin Klein sectional from the truck.

"That's enough honking, dear. It's early!" Glory swatted her husband playfully. "The neighbors are going to think we're lunatics."

The smell of coffee breath and cardboard to-go cups made Melody's empty stomach lurch.

"Yeah, Dad, *stawp*," Candace moaned, her head still resting on her metallic Tory Burch bag. "You're wakey-waking the only cool person in Salem."

Beau unclipped his seat belt and turned to face his daughter. "And who might that be?"

"Meeee." Candace stretched, her chest rising and then sinking inside her light blue tank like a buoy on a choppy sea. She must have fallen asleep on her angry, balled-up fist, because her cheek was imprinted with the heart from her new ring—the one her teary best friends gave her as a going-away present.

Melody, desperate to dodge the *I-miss-my-friends* bullet Candace would undoubtedly fire when she noticed her cheek, was the first to open the door and step onto the winding street.

The rain had stopped and the sun was rising. A purplish red layer of mist cloaked the neighborhood like a thin fuchsia scarf over a lampshade. It cast a magical glow over Radcliffe Way. Damp and glistening, the neighborhood smelled like earthworms and wet grass.

"Get a whiff of that air, Melly." Beau smacked his flannel-covered lungs and lifted his head in reverence to the tie-dyed sky.

"I know." Melody hugged his corrugated abs. "I can breathe

better already," she assured him, partly because she wanted him to know she appreciated his sacrifice but mostly because she truly could breathe more easily. It felt as if a sandbag had been lifted from her chest.

"You gotta get out and smell this," Beau insisted, tapping his wife's window with his gold initial ring.

Glory lifted her finger impatiently and then cocked her head toward Candace, in the backseat, to show she was dealing with another meltdown.

"Sorry." Melody hugged her father again, this time with a softer grip, a grip that begged *forgive me*.

"For what? This is great!" He took a long, deep breath. "The Carvers needed a change. We had LA dialed. It's time for a new challenge. Living is all about—"

"I wish I was dead!" Candace screamed from inside the SUV.

"There goes the only cool person in Salem," Beau mumbled under his breath.

Melody looked up at her father. The instant their eyes met, they burst out laughing.

"All right, who's ready for a tour?" Glory opened the door. The tip of her fur-lined hiking bootie lowered tentatively toward the pavement as if testing the temperature of a bath.

Candace jumped out from the backseat. "First one upstairs gets the big room!" she shouted, and then charged toward the house. Her toothpick legs moved at an impressive clip, unencumbered by the Speedo tightness of her fashionably torn skinny jeans.

Melody shot her mother a quick *how'd-you-do-that?* look.

"I told her she could have my vintage Missoni jumpsuit if she stopped complaining for the rest of the day," Glory confessed, gathering her auburn hair into an elegant ponytail and securing it with a quick twist.

"With promises like that, you'll be down to one sock by the end of the week," Beau teased.

"It'll be worth it." Glory smiled.

Melody giggled and then took off toward the house. She knew Candace would beat her to the big room. But that's not why she was running. She was running because after so many years of labored breathing, she finally could.

Bounding past the trucks, she nodded at the men struggling with the couch. Then she leaped up the three wood steps to the front door.

"No *way*!" Melody gasped, stopping at the foot of the spacious cabin. The walls had the same orange-hued Lincoln Logs as the outside. So did the steps, the banister, the ceiling, and the railings. The only deviations were the stone fireplace and the walnut floors. It was hardly what she was used to, considering they came from a multitiered glass-and-concrete homage to ultramodern design. But Melody had to admire her parents. They were certainly committed to this new outdoor-lifestyle thing.

"Behind you," grunted a sweat-soaked mover trying to negotiate the plump couch through the narrow doorway.

"Oops, sorry." Melody giggled nervously, stepping aside.

To her right, a long bedroom spanned the entire length of the house. Beau and Glory's California king was already inside holding court, and the master bath was in the middle of a major facelift. A tinted sliding glass door opened onto a narrow lap pool that was enclosed by an eight-foot-high Lincoln Log wall. The indoor pool must have sealed the deal for Beau, who swam every morning to burn off the calories his nightly swim might have missed.

Overhead, in one of the remaining two bedrooms, Candace was pacing and mumbling into her phone.

Across from her parents' room was a cozy kitchen and dining area. The Carvers' sleek appliances, glass table, and eight black-lacquered chairs looked futuristic compared to the rustic wood. But Melody was sure the situation would be remedied as soon as her mom and dad located the nearest design center.

"Help!" Candace called from upstairs.

"Huh?" Melody called back, peeking at the sunken living room and its view of the wooded ravine out back.

"I'm dying!"

"*Really?*" Melody bounded up the wooden staircase in the middle of the cabin. She loved the way the uneven wood slabs felt beneath her black Converse high-tops. Each one had its own unique personality. It wasn't a celebration of symmetry, cohesion, and perfection, like Beverly Hills. It was the exact opposite. Every log in the house had its own patterns and nicks. Each was unique. None was perfect. Yet they all fit together and supported a single vision. Maybe it was a regional thing. Maybe all Salemites (Salemonians? Salemers?) celebrated unique patterns and nicks. And if *they* did, that meant the students at Merston High did too. The possibility filled her with a burst of asthma-free hope that propelled her up the steps, two at a time.

At the top, Melody unzipped her black hoodie and threw it over the railing. The pits of her gray Hanes tee were soaked with sweat, and her forehead was beading up.

"I'm dying. It's so seriously *fuego*." Candace appeared from the bedroom on the left wearing nothing but a black bra and jeans. "Is it two hundred degrees in here, or am I going through the change?"

"Candi." Melody tossed her the hoodie. "Put this on!"

"Why?" she asked, casually inspecting her belly button. "Our windows are limo-tinted. It's not like anyone can see inside."

"Um, how 'bout the *movers*?" Melody snapped.

Candace pressed the hoodie against her chest and then peered over the railing. "This place is kinda weird, don'tcha think?" The flush in her cheeks burned straight up to her aqua blue eyes, giving them an iridescent glow.

"This whole house is weird," Melody whispered. "I kinda love it."

"That's because *you're* weird." Candace whipped the hoodie over the railing and sauntered into what must have been the bigger bedroom. A sassy mass of blond hair swung across her back as if waving good-bye.

"Someone lose a top?" called one of the movers from down below. The black garment was slumped over his shoulder like a dead ferret.

"Um, yeah, sorry," Melody answered. "You can just throw it on the steps." She hurried to the only remaining bedroom so he wouldn't think she was hitting on him.

She looked around the small rectangular space: log walls, low ceiling with deep scratches that looked like claw marks, a tinted mini window that revealed a view of the next-door neighbor's stone fence. The closet smelled like cedar when its sliding door was opened. The temperature in the room must have been close to five hundred degrees. A real-estate listing would call it "cozy" if the agent wasn't afraid to lie.

"Nice coffin," Candace, still dressed in her bra, teased from the doorway.

"Nice *try*," Melody countered. "I still don't want to move back."

"Fine." Candace rolled her eyes. "Then at least let me make you jealous. Check out my boudoir."

Melody followed her sister past the cramped bathroom and into a spacious, light-filled square. It had an alcove for a desk, three deep closets, and an expansive tinted window overlooking Radcliffe Way. They could have shared it and still had room for Candace's ego.

"Cute," Melody muttered, trying not to sound the least bit envious. "Hey, wanna walk into town and get some bagels or something? I'm starving."

"Not until you admit that my room rocks and you're jealous." Candace folded her arms across her chest.

"No way."

Candace turned toward her window in protest. "Um, how about *now*?" She blew a fog circle with her breath and then finger-drew a heart inside.

Melody proceeded with caution. "Is this some kind of setup?"

"You wish," Candace said, eyeing the bare-chested boy in the garden across the street.

He was watering the yellow roses in front of a white cottage, wielding the hose like a sword. Lean back muscles undulated every time he thrust forward to joust. His worn jeans had slipped just enough to reveal the elastic band on his striped boxers.

"Is that the gardener, or do you think he lives there?" Melody asked.

"Lives there," Candace said with certainty. "If he was a gardener, he'd be tanned. Tie me."

"Huh?"

Melody turned to find her sister dressed in a purple, black, and silver zigzagged Missoni jumpsuit, holding the halter straps behind her head.

"How did you find that?" Melody asked, tying a perfect bow. "The wardrobe boxes are still on the truck."

"I knew Mom would give it to me if I kept complaining, so I snuck it in my bag before we left."

"So all of that stuff in the car was an act?" Melody's heart began to trot.

"Pretty much." Candace shrugged casually. "I'll make friends and meet guys wherever. Besides, I need to keep my grades up this year if I want to get into a good college. And we all know that wasn't gonna happen senior year in Cali."

Melody wasn't sure whether she wanted to hug her sister or hit her. But there wasn't time for either.

Candace had already slipped on a pair of Glory's silver platform sandals and scuttled back to the window. "Now, who's ready to meet the neighbors?"

"Candace, don't!" Melody begged, but her sister was already struggling with the iron latch. Trying to tame Candace was like trying to stop a moving roller coaster by waving your hands in the air. It was an exhausting waste of time.

"Hey, Hot Stuff!" Candace shouted out the window, then ducked below the ledge.

The boy turned and looked up, sheltering his eyes from the sun.

Candace lifted her head and peeked. "Nope. Not interested," she muttered. "Too young. Four eyes. No tan. You can have him."

Melody wanted to shout "I don't need you to tell me who I can and can't *have*!" But there was a shirtless boy with black-framed glasses and a mop of brown hair staring at her. All she could do was stare back and wonder what color his eyes were.

He waved awkwardly, but Melody remained frozen. Maybe he'd assume she was one of those life-size cardboard cutouts in the lobby of the movie theater and not a really socially awkward girl who was about to kick her sister in the shin.

"Ouch!" Candace wailed, grabbing her shin.

Melody moved away from the window. "I can't believe you did that to me," she whisper-shouted.

"Well it's not like *you* were going to do anything," Candace insisted, her blue-green eyes widening from the strength of her own conviction.

"Why would I? I don't even know him." Melody leaned against the bumpy log wall and lowered her head in her hands.

"So?"

"Sooooo, I'm tired of people thinking I'm a freak. I know *you* can't relate to that but—"

"Get over it already, will ya?" Candace stood. "You're not Smellody anymore. You're *pretty*. You can get *hot* guys now. Tanned ones with good vision. Not geeky hose jousters." She shut the window. "Don't you ever want to use your lips as something other than veneer protectors?"

Melody felt a familiar pinch behind her eyes. Her throat dried. Her mouth twitched. Her eyes burned. And then they came. Like salty little paratroopers, tears descended en masse. She hated that Candace thought she had never made out with a boy. But how could she convince a seventeen-year-old with more dates than a fruitcake that Randy the Starbucks cashier (aka Scarbucks, because of his acne scars) was a great kisser? She couldn't.

"It's not that simple, okay?" Melody kept her tear-soaked face hidden. "Being pretty is your dream. Singing *was* mine. And it's over."

"So live my dream for a while." Candace swiped gloss across her lips. "It's more fun than feeling sorry for yourself, that's for sure."

How could Melody possibly explain her feelings to Candace when she barely understood them herself? "My pretty is fake, Candace. It was engineered. It's not even *me*."

Candace rolled her eyes.

"How would you feel if you got an A on a test that you copied off someone?" Melody asked, trying another tactic.

"Depends," Candace said. "Did I get caught?"

Melody lifted her head and laughed. A giant snot bubble burst on her nose, which she quickly wiped on her jeans before her sister could see.

"You think about this stuff too much." Candace swung her purse over her shoulder and then glanced down at her cleavage. "I've never looked better." She held out her hand and pulled Melody to her feet. "It's time to teach the good people of Salem the difference between Carhartt and couture." After a quick scan of Melody's sweaty gray Hanes T-shirt and baggy jeans, she added, "Just let me do all the talking."

"I always do." Melody sighed.

24

CHAPTER FOUR
MINT CONDITION

Frankie jumped to her bare feet and began dancing to the Lady Gaga beats lingering inside her head.

"So you're okay with going to school?" Viveka's spidery black lashes fluttered with disbelief.

"Completely!" Frankie swung her hands above her head and snap-twirled. "I get to make friends! I get to meet boys! I get to sit in a cafeteria! I get to go outside and—"

"Hold on a minute," Viktor interrupted, serious as science. "It's not that simple."

"You're right!" Frankie bolted toward her sky-blue wardrobe; the one tagged SKIRTS AND DRESSES in fuchsia spray paint. "What am I going to wear?"

"This." Viktor leaned forward, placed the leather duffel at her feet, and then quickly backed away, as if offering a side salad to a hungry lion.

Instantly, Frankie changed course and headed toward the bag. It was so like her parents to get her a first-day-of-school outfit. *Is it the pleated bebe mini with the black cashmere tank? Oh, please make it the pleated bebe mini with the black cashmere tank. Oh pleaseohpleaseohpleaseohpleaseohplease!*

She unzipped the bag and reached inside, feeling around for the soft straps and cute oversize pin that held the kilt closed.

"Ouch!" She pulled her hand out of the bag as though it had teeth. "What was *that?*" she asked, still reeling from brushing up against the coarse object inside.

"It's a sharp wool pantsuit." Viveka gathered her hair and flung it over one shoulder.

"Sharp is right!" Frankie countered. "It feels like a cheese grater."

"It's darling," Viveka pressed. "Try it on."

Frankie turned the bag upside down to avoid touching the abrasive garment. A large chocolate-brown makeup case plopped onto the rug. "What's that?"

"Makeup," Viktor declared.

"From Sephora?" Frankie asked hopefully, giving her parents the chance to redeem themselves.

"No." Viktor ran a hand over the comb tracks in his slicked-back hair. "From New York City. It's a wonderful line of stage makeup called Fierce & Flawless, meant to hold up under the brightest theater lights on Broadway. Yet, it's not too heavy." Viktor pulled a soap-filled pad from the bag and scrubbed his forearm. A pinkish-yellow smudge was on the pad. A green streak was on his arm.

Frankie gasped. "You have mint skin too?"

"So do I." Viveka scrubbed a similar streak across her cheek.

"*What?*" Frankie's hands sparked. "Have you always been mint?"

They nodded proudly.

"Then why do you cover it up?"

"Because"—Viktor wiped his finger on the leg of his tracksuit—"we live in a world of normies. And many of them are afraid of people who look different."

"Different from *what?*" Frankie wondered aloud.

Viktor looked down. "Different from them."

"We are part of a very special group descended from what normies call monsters," Viveka explained. "But we like to refer to ourselves as RADs."

"Regular Attribute Dodgers," Viktor clarified.

Frankie reached for her neck stitches.

"Don't pull!" her parents said together.

Frankie lowered her hand and sighed. "Has it always been like this?"

"Not *always*." Viktor stood. He began to pace. "Unfortunately, our history, like that of so many others, is full of periods of persecution. But we had finally moved beyond the Middle Ages and were living openly among the normies. We worked together, socialized together, and fell in love with each other. But in the 1920s and '30s, all that changed."

"Why?" Frankie crawled onto the couch and snuggled up to Viveka. The smell of her mother's gardenia body oil comforted her.

"Horror movies took off. RADs were being cast to star in all kinds of films, like *Dracula*, *Phantom of the Opera*, *Dr. Jekyll and Mr. Hyde*. And the ones who couldn't act—"

"Like your grandpa Vic," Viveka teased.

"Yes, like dear old Victor Frankenstein." He chuckled, recalling a memory. "He had a problem memorizing his lines and, truth be told, he was quite stiff. So he was portrayed by a normie actor named Boris Karloff."

"Sounds fun." Frankie twirled her finger around the silky tie on her robe, wishing she had been alive back then.

"It *was*." Viktor stopped pacing and looked straight at her, his grin fading like dusk. "Until the movies were released."

"Why?" Frankie asked.

"They portrayed us as horrifying, evil, bloodsucking enemies of the people." Viktor paced again. "Normie children screamed in terror when they saw us. Their parents stopped inviting us into their homes. And no one would do business with us. We became outcasts overnight. RADs experienced violence and vandalism. Our life as we knew it was over."

"Didn't anyone fight back?" Frankie asked, recalling the many historical battles waged for similar reasons.

"We tried." Viktor shook his head, mourning the failed attempt. "Protests were pointless. They turned into frenzied autograph sessions for fearless horror fans. And any action stronger than a protest would have made us look like the angry beasts the normies feared we were."

"So what did everyone do?" Frankie curled up closer to her mother.

"A secret alert was sent out to all the RADs urging them to leave their homes and businesses and meet up in Salem, where the witches lived. The hope was that the witches would identify with our struggles and take us in. Together we could form a new community and start fresh."

"But didn't the Salem witch trials get rid of all the witches, in like, 1692? And wasn't this the 1930s?" Frankie asked.

Viktor clapped his hands once and then pointed at his daughter like an effusive game show host. "That's right!" he gushed, taking pride in his daughter's implanted book smarts.

Viveka kissed Frankie's head. "Too bad the brainless zombie who sent the alert wasn't as smart as you."

"Yeah." Viktor smoothed his hair. "Not only were the witches long gone, but he got the wrong Salem. He was thinking of Salem, Massachusetts, but he gave the coordinates for Salem, Oregon. All the RADs realized his mistake, but there was no time to change course. They had to get out before they were rounded up and thrown in jail.

"When they arrived in Oregon, they decided to just make the best of it. They pooled their money, disguised themselves as normies, built Radcliffe Way, and vowed to protect one another. The hope is that someday we'll be able to live openly again, but until that time comes, it's crucial that we blend in. Being discovered would force us into exile again. Our homes, careers, and lifestyles would be destroyed."

"That's why it's important that you cover your skin and hide your bolts and seams," Viveka explained.

"Where are yours?" Frankie asked.

Viveka lifted her black scarf and winked. Two shiny bolts winked back.

Viktor unzipped the high collar on his track jacket, revealing his hardware.

"*Vol*-tage," Frankie whispered, awestruck.

"I'm going to get breakfast started." Viveka stood and smoothed the wrinkles in her dress. "The makeup comes with an instructional DVD," she explained. "You should start practicing now."

Her parents each kissed her on the forehead and then started to close the door behind them.

Viveka peeked back in. "Remember," she said, "you want to have this down by the time school starts." Then she gently shut the door.

"Okay." Frankie smiled, remembering that this downer of a conversation had begun on a total high. She was going to *school*!

Frankie flexed her toes and kicked away an unsightly pile of wool clothing as if it were a dead squirrel. No one was wearing wool pantsuits this season, she thought, as the itchy offenders skittered out of her line of vision.

Just to be certain, she consulted *Teen Vogue*'s back-to-school issue. As she had suspected, this year was all about light fabrics, jewel tones, and animal prints. Scarves and chunky jewelry were the must-have accessories. Wool was so out, it didn't even make the "out" list.

The articles were extremely eye-opening. Not just in *Teen Vogue* but in *Seventeen* and *CosmoGirl* as well. They all were about being yourself, staying natural, loving your body as is, and going green! The messages were the exact opposite of Vik and Viv's.

Hmmmm.

Frankie turned to face the full-length mirror that was propped up against the yellow wardrobe. She opened her robe and examined her body. Fit, muscular, and exquisitely proportioned, she agreed with the magazines. So what if her skin was mint? Or her limbs were attached with seams? According to the magazines, which were—no offense!—way more in touch with the times than her parents were, she was supposed to love her body just the way it was. And she did! Therefore, if the normies read magazines (which obviously they did, because they were in them), then they would love her too. Natural was *in*.

Besides, she was Daddy's perfect little girl. And who didn't love perfect?

CHAPTER FIVE
THE PICKUP ARTIST

Despite the early hour, Melody and Candace took to Radcliffe Way with the boundless energy of two girls who had been cooped up in an SUV for fourteen hours. Surprisingly, their new neighborhood was abuzz with activity. At the end of the street kids circled the cul-de-sac on their bikes, and a few doors down an entire family of jocks was playing football in the front yard.

"Is that *one* family?" Melody asked as they approached the cavernous stone house, where no fewer than ten boys were charging the shaggy-haired hottie with the ball.

"The parents must have had multiples," Candace noted while fluffing her hair.

Suddenly, the game slowed, and then stopped, while the pack watched the Carver sisters stroll by.

"Why is everyone staring at us?" Melody mumbled from the side of her mouth.

"Get used to it," Candace mumbled back. "People stare when you're pretty." She smile-waved at the high school–age boys, each with his own adorable mess of shaggy brown hair and a maybe-it's-Maybelline cheek flush. Smoke from their Hummer-size grill circulated the tangy smell of barbecued ribs through the neighborhood at a time when most people hadn't finished their first cup of coffee.

Melody gripped her hollow stomach. Dinner for breakfast sounded great right about now.

"I loved you in last month's J.Crew catalog," Candace called out.

The boys exchanged confused looks.

"Candace!" Melody smacked her sister's arm.

"Have some fun, will ya?" Candace laughed, clicking along the pavement in her mother's silver platforms.

"Everyone we pass looks at us like we're from another planet."

"We *are*." Candace tightened the neck straps on her Missoni jumpsuit.

"Maybe it's because you're wearing Saturday night on a Sunday morning."

"I'm pretty sure it's because you're wearing yesterday's road trip *today*," Candace snapped. "Nothing says make new friends like a sweaty gray Hanes T-shirt and baggy jeans."

Melody considered retaliating but didn't bother. It wouldn't change anything. Candace would always believe that good looks were a skeleton key for success. And Melody would always hope that people were deeper than that.

They walked along the rest of Radcliffe Way in silence. The winding road cut through some kind of forest or ravine—the homes on both sides had grassy front yards and dense, woodsy thickets for backyards. But that's where the similarities ended. Like the uniquely marked logs in the Carver cabin, each house had defining features that made it individual.

A gray concrete slab in the cul-de-sac was fenced in by an unsightly tangle of electrical wires and phone lines. An old Victorian was completely shaded under a canopy of big-leaf maples and had an endless flurry of propeller-like seeds that helicoptered to the mossy ground. A black-bottomed swimming pool and dozens of mini sea-creature fountains provided tons of fun for everyone at No. 9. Even though the sun was tucked away under a duvet of silver-colored clouds, the neighbors were out swimming, splashing around like a school of playful dolphins.

It was becoming more and more evident that Salem was a town that celebrated individuality, a real live-and-let-live kind of place. Melody felt a gut punch of regret. Her old nose would have fit in here.

"Look!" She pointed at the multicolored car whizzing by. Its black doors were from a Mercedes coupe, the white hood from a BMW; the silver trunk was Jaguar, the red convertible top was Lexus, the whitewall tires were Bentley, the sound system Bose, and the music was classical. A hood ornament from each model dangled from the rearview mirror. Its license plate appropriately read MUTT.

"That car looks like a moving Benetton ad."

"Or a pileup on Rodeo Drive." Candace snapped a picture with her iPhone and e-mailed it to her friends back home. They responded instantly with a shot of what they were doing. It must have involved the mall because Candace picked up her pace once they turned onto Staghorn Road and began asking anyone under the age of fifty where the cool people hung out.

The answer was unanimous: the Riverfront. But it wouldn't be hopping for a few more hours.

After a leisurely latte stop and several pauses to peer into clothing stores (deemed "unshoppable" by Candace), it was finally pushing noon. With the help of Beau's map and the kindness of strangers, the girls navigated their way through the sleepy town and arrived at the Riverfront—fully caffeinated and ready to announce their presence to the cool people of Salem.

"This is *it*?" Candace stopped short, as if she had hit a pane of glass. "This is the epicenter of Northwest chic?" she shouted at the snow cone cart, the children's playground, and the brick building that housed a carousel.

"Mmmmmm, I smell movie theater lobby," Melody announced, sniffing the air scented with popcorn and hot dogs.

"You can take the nose out of Smellody," Candace cracked, "but you can't take Smellody out of the nose."

"Very funny." Melody rolled her eyes.

"No, actually, it's not!" Candace huffed. "None of this is very funny at all. In fact, it's a total nightmare. *Listen!*" She pointed at the carousel. Manic organ music—a must for horror movie sound tracks and psycho clown scenes—mocked them with its menacingly playful lilt.

"The only person over the age of eight and under the age of forty is that dude over there." Candace pointed at a lone boy on a wooden bench. "And I think he's crying."

His shoulders were hunched, and his head hung over a sketch pad. He lifted his eyes for quick glimpses of the spinning carousel, then went right back to scribbling.

Melody's armpits prickled with sweat, her body recognizing

him before her brain did. "Let's get out of here," she said, tugging Candace's thin arm.

But it was too late. Her sister's lips curled with delight, and her platforms held firm to the gum-spotted pavement. "Is that—"

"No! Let's just go," Melody insisted, tugging harder. "I think I saw a Bloomingdale's back there. Come on."

"It is!" Candace dragged Melody toward the boy. Beaming, she called out, "Hey, neighbor!"

He lifted his head and then smacked a chunk of wavy brown hair away from his face. Melody's stomach lurched. He was even cuter up close.

Thick black glasses surrounded his crackling hazel eyes, making them look like framed photos of lightning in a dark sky. He had the geek-chic look of a disguised superhero.

"You remember my sister from the window, don't you?" Candace asked with a trace of revenge, as if it were Melody's fault the Riverfront was a bust.

"Um, hey...I'm...Melody," she managed, cheeks burning.

"Jackson." He lowered his eyes.

Candace pinched his white crew-neck tee. "We almost didn't recognize you with your shirt on."

Jackson smiled nervously; his eyes fixed uncomfortably on his drawing.

"You're kinda *curdy*," Candace cooed, as if her contraction for *cute-nerdy* was actual English. "Any chance you have an older brother with good vision...or contacts?" she pressed.

"Nope." Jackson's clear, pale skin reddened. "Just me."

Melody pressed her arms against her body to hide the pit sweat. "What are you drawing?" she asked. It wasn't the most exciting question, but it was better than anything Candace was going to say.

Jackson consulted his sketch pad as if seeing it for the first time. "It's just the carousel. You know, while it's moving."

Melody examined the blur of pastels. Inside the smudged rainbow were subtle outlines of horses and children. It had a gauzy, elusive quality to it—like the haunting memory of a dream, appearing and disappearing in fractured flashes throughout the day. "That's really good," she said, meaning it. "Have you been doing it long?"

Jackson shrugged. "'Bout a half hour. I'm just waiting for my mom. She had a meeting around here, so..."

Melody giggled. "No, I meant have you been drawing long. You know, as a hobby."

"Oh." Jackson ran a hand through his hair. The choppy layers fell right back into place like cards being shuffled. "Yeah, you know, a few years."

"Nice." Melody nodded.

"Yeah." Jackson nodded back.

"Cool." Melody nodded again.

"Thanks." Jackson nodded back.

"Sure." Melody nodded.

The organ music blaring from the carousel suddenly sounded louder. Like it was trying to save them from their monosyllabic bobble-heading by offering a distraction.

"So, uh, where are you from?" Jackson asked Candace, eyeing her out-of-state outfit.

"Beverly Hills," she said, like it should have been obvious.

"We moved here because of my asthma," Melody announced.

"Real sexy, Mel." Candace sighed, giving up.

"Well, it's *true*."

Jackson's tight features unwound into a comfortable smile. It was as if Melody's admission had asked his confidence to dance. And it had said yes.

"So, um, have you heard of Merston High?" she asked, her words providing the necessary music.

"Yeah." He slid over, silently offering half the bench. "I go there."

Melody sat down, her arms still pressed against her sides in case she was downwind. "What grade?"

Candace stood above them, texting.

"Starting tenth."

"Same." Melody smiled more than she needed to.

"Really?" Jackson smiled back. Or, rather, his smile was still there from before.

Melody nodded. "So, what are the people like? Are they cool?"

Jackson lowered his eyes and then shrugged. His smile faded. The music had stopped. Their dance was over. The oily smell of his pastels lingered like a crush's cologne.

"*What?*" Melody asked sadly, her heart thumping a woeful dirge.

"The people are fine, I guess. It's just that my mom's the science teacher and she's pretty strict, so I'm not exactly on anyone's speed dial."

"You can be on mine," Melody offered sweetly.

"Really?" Jackson asked, his forehead starting to glow with sweat.

Melody nodded, her heart now thumping a livelier beat. She felt surprisingly comfortable with this stranger. Maybe because he wasn't simply looking *at* her face; he was looking *through* it. And he didn't stop just because she wore sweaty road trip clothes and told curdy boys she had asthma.

"Okay." He studied her face one last time and then scribbled his cell number on his sketch with a red pastel. "Here." He tore the sheet from the pad, handed it to her, and then quickly wiped his brow with the back of his hand. "I better go."

"Okay," Melody stood when he stood, lifted by the strength of their connection.

"See you around." He waved awkwardly, turned toward the whirling carousel, and hurried away.

"Nicely played." Candace dropped her phone in her metallic bag. "Curdy boys are great practice. Now let's go find something to eat." She quickly scanned the park. "There's got to be something around here that won't give us salmonella."

Melody followed Candace over the meandering walkways, grinning at the red phone number. Asking for it was one thing. Working up the nerve to call would be quite another. Still, she had it. He had given it to her. *Willingly.* Thereby permitting her to replay the details of their conversation in her head as many times as she wanted without wondering whether the attraction was one-sided.

And so she would.

"How about a hot dog bun and a Diet Coke?" Candace suggested.

"I'll pass." Melody grinned at the beautiful cloud-covered sky. She was no longer feeling the least bit empty.

CHAPTER SIX
NOTHING IS AS IT SEAMS

Viveka knocked on the door to Frankie's Fab. "Let's go! We're going to be late!"

"Coming!" Frankie called in reply, just as she had the previous four times. But what she really wanted to say was "You can't rush perfection." Because the outfit she was modeling for the Glitterati was indeed perfection. Or it would be, as soon as she chose a pair of sunglasses.

"Do you like the white?" she put on some oversize plastic frames, then struck a hand-on-hip chin-jut pose. "Or the green?" An erupted volcano of clothing covered the floor, making it hard for her to walk and spin for the white lab rats, especially in metallic pink super-wedges. But the rats could grasp the idea without all the pomp and circumstance. After all, they had been collaborating for the last three hours. And they'd done a pretty fine job so far. Scratching once for yes and twice for no, they had nominated her black-and-white striped tank with the floral mini. Mixing patterns was very current.

"White or green?" Frankie asked again.

Three rats lay curled in an exhausted heap. The remaining two, however, scratched once for white. A solid choice, because the green wasn't exactly popping against her skin, and blending in was the last thing she wanted to do on her first day of normie school.

She pulled her black hair up in a high-swinging ponytail, glossed her full lips, and rubbed a magazine sample of Estée Lauder Sensuous perfume over her neck bolts. Because, as the ad copy said, "every woman wears it her way."

"Wish me luck, Glitterati!" She kissed the glass cage, leaving behind a shiny pink lip print.

The remaining two rats collapsed in the heap of fur and sparkles.

"Ready!" Frankie announced.

Her parents were standing at the stainless-steel island in the kitchen, alternating bites of the same bagel and speed-drinking their coffee—something they did to practice being normal. Because, like Frankie, they charged and didn't need to eat.

The L-shaped home, with its sharp edges and minimalist's penchant for white, had the electricity smell of burned toast and the ammonia smell of efficiency. The morning light approached the frosted windows, searching for a way inside.

Everything was as it had always been, yet at the same time it was all so different. Alive. Cheerful. Charged. Because, for the first time in her life, Frankie was allowed to leave the house.

"You're not going anywhere dressed like that!" Viktor slammed his white coffee mug on the open newspaper.

"Frankie, where's the pantsuit?" Viveka marched over to her

daughter. Her mother's makeup, gray turtleneck sweater dress, black leggings, and over-the-knee boots took on a whole new meaning now that Frankie knew the truth.

"Why aren't you wearing your Fierce & Flawless?" Viktor boomed.

"Go *green*!" Frankie preached, just like the magazines. "That's one of the biggest messages of our time. Besides, I'm proud of who I am and how you made me. And if people don't like me because I'm not a normie, then that's their problem, not mine."

"You are *not* leaving the house like that." Viktor held firm. "Not with your seams and bolts hanging out."

"Dad!" Sparks flew from Frankie's fingertips. "Pantsuits are where fabric goes to die." She stomped her wedge on the white carpet. Unfortunately, the dense shag muffled her frustration and failed to express her urgency.

"Your father is right," Viveka insisted.

Frankie glared at her cookie dough–colored parents breathing to the condescending rhythm of their mutual obstinacy.

"Go," Viktor demanded, "before we're all late."

Frankie stomped off to her bedroom. She emerged seconds later wearing a brown scarf and leather wrist cuffs, but only because *Teen Vogue* had endorsed them as must-have accessories for fall. She smirked. "There. The seams and bolts are covered. Can we go now?"

Viveka and Viktor exchanged a glance and then made their way to the side door that connected to the garage. Frankie followed behind in her totally voltage outfit and victory grin. She was on the fast track to fabulous.

Beepboop. The doors to the black Volvo SUV unlocked.

"Let's take MUTT!" she suggested, cherishing an implanted memory of a family drive to Silver Falls and wanting to experience it for real.

"I think we should take something less conspicuous," Viktor insisted.

"But, Dad, DIY is so popular," Frankie explained. "And MUTT is DIY car-sonified. Everyone at school will love it."

"*Car-sonified* is not a word, Frankie!" her father said sternly. "And we're through negotiating."

The ride to school was endlessly boring. The trees, cars, homes, and even normies that she saw outside the tinted windows looked no different in real life than they did in her simulated memories. The big thrill was going to be breathing fresh air. But open windows were strictly forbidden because she wasn't coated in Fierce & Flawless. So breathing would have to wait.

After a two-hour drive, the black Volvo finally arrived at Mount Hood High. Frankie couldn't believe there wasn't a closer school, but she didn't dare say a word. Her parents were already irritated, and she worried that another disagreement might land her back at home.

Barely bothering to look at the regal mountain in the background or the red and yellow leaves that drifted aimlessly from the trees, Frankie stepped out of the car and took her first real sniff of air. Crisp, cool, and free of formaldehyde, it smelled like spring water in a bowl of soil. She took off her white sunglasses and lifted her green face to the sky. Unfiltered sun hugged and warmed her skin. Her eyes teared from the glare. Or was it the joy?

It didn't matter that Frankie had no idea where to go. Or that she had never ventured away from her parents before. They had filled her with so much knowledge and confidence, she had no doubt she would find her way. And she'd enjoy trying.

It was odd to see the campus bare, with so few cars in the parking lot. She was tempted to ask her parents where everyone was, but she decided against it. Why make them think she wasn't ready?

"Are you sure you don't want makeup?" Viveka asked, her head poking out the passenger-side window.

"Positive," Frankie assured her. The sun on her arms felt more energizing than Carmen Electra. "See you after school." She smiled, air-kissing them good-bye before they had empty-nest meltdowns. "Good luck with your first day back at work."

"Thanks," they answered, together, of course.

Frankie strolled toward the main doors, sniffing the air like she was at an all-you-can-breathe buffet. She could feel their eyes tracking her across the empty parking lot, but she refused to look back. From this moment on, it was all about moving forward.

She climbed eleven wide steps to the double doors, enjoying the aching sensation real-life exercise was bringing to her legs. *Feeling* it was so different from simply knowing about it.

After a quick pause to catch her breath, Frankie reached for the handle of the door and—

"*Oof!*" The door smacked her in the cheek. Bolts sparking, she covered her throbbing face with her hand and lowered her head.

"Oh no! Are you okay?" asked a gaggle of girls in varying tones. They had crowded around her like the New York City skyline. A medley of perfumes chased away Frankie's fresh air and left behind a fruit-scented bout of nausea.

43

"It was a total accident," said one of them, stroking Frankie's high ponytail. "We didn't see you. Can you see?"

The friendly gesture bathed Frankie in more warmth than the sun. Normies were nice! "I'm okay." She smiled and looked up. "It was more shocking than painful, you know?"

"What the *Shrek*…is that?" A blond in a yellow-and-green cheerleader outfit backed away.

"Either you're majorly carsick or your skin is…*green*," another blond noted.

"Is this a joke?" asked another one, backing away just in case.

"No, it really is mint." She smiled humbly and extended her arm for a friendly shake. Her cuff slid forward, revealing a row of wrist seams, but Frankie didn't really care. This is who she was. Bolts and all. "I'm new here. My name is Frankie and I'm from—"

"The Build-A-Bear Workshop?" one of them asked, slowly moving away.

"Monster!" yelled the only brunette. She pulled a cell phone out of her bra, dialed 911, and ran into the school.

"Ahhhhhhh!" the others screamed, wiggling their limbs as though they were covered in bugs.

"I told you it was bad luck to practice on a Sunday!" one of them sobbed.

The girls darted back through the doors and jammed chairs against them with floor-scraping urgency.

Sunday?

Sirens wailed in the distance. The black Volvo skidded to a halt at the bottom of the steps, and Viktor jumped out.

"Hurry!" Viveka called from the open window.

Mind blank and body frozen, Frankie watched her father run toward her. "Let's get out of here!" he shouted.

The sirens were getting closer.

"I wanted to teach you a lesson," he mumbled, lifting his daughter and carrying her to safety. "But I never should have let it go this far."

Frankie burst into tears as her father sped out of the parking lot and turned, tires screeching onto Balsam Avenue. The Volvo merged with traffic just as a slew of police cars pulled up and surrounded the school.

"Just in time," Viveka uttered softly, and tears began to roll down her face.

Viktor's attention lay solely on the road ahead. His squint was unwavering, and his thin lips were sealed shut. There was no need for an *I-told-you-so* lecture. Or even an apology from Frankie. It was clear what had happened and obvious what each one of them could have done differently. Only one question remained: What now?

Frankie glared at her tear-soaked face reflected in the car window. The ugly truth glared back. Her looks were frightening.

One by one, drops fell from her eyes like they were on an assembly line—gather, fall, slide…gather, fall, slide…each one commemorating something she had lost. Hope. Faith. Confidence. Pride. Security. Trust. Independence. Joy. Beauty. Freedom. Innocence.

Her father turned on the radio.

"…alleged monster sighting at Mount Hood High has four cheerleaders in a state of absolute panic." News had traveled fast.

"Turn it off, Viktor," Viveka said, sniffing.

"It's important to know what they know," he said, turning up the volume. "We need to assess the damage."

Frankie sparked.

"...Tell us exactly what you saw," said the deep male voice on the radio.

"She was green—at least, I think she was a she. But it was hard to tell. It all happened so fast. One minute it was pretending to be human, and the next it was reaching for us like some kind of"—the girl's voice began to quake—"alien *beeeeeastttttttt!*"

Frankie's sadness froze into anger. "I was trying to introduce myself!"

"You're safe now," the interviewer said, trying to comfort the witness. "Why don't you take a minute," he suggested, his voice temporarily trailing off.

When he returned, he was all business. "Salem had its first monster sighting back in 1940," he explained, "when a pack of werewolves was apprehended at the California-Oregon border holding McDonald's bags in between their teeth. Things were peaceful again until 2007, when a boy named Billy began disappearing and reappearing right before people's eyes. And now a green alien beast has been spotted at Mount Hood High...."

Viveka snapped off the radio. "At least they're looking for an alien." She sighed, relieved.

"Frankie"—Viktor met his daughter's eyes in the rearview mirror—"classes start Tuesday. After Labor Day. At your real school. It's called Merston High, and it's three blocks from our house. But we won't let you go unless—"

"I know. I get it." Frankie sniffed. "I'll wear everything. I promise." She meant it. Her desire to go green was gone.

CHAPTER SEVEN
FRIEND-FREE ZONE

The lunchtime bell *bwoopbwoop*ed like a European busy signal. The inaugural morning at Merston High was officially over. It was no longer a mysterious place in Melody's imagination, filled with endless possibilities and hooks on which to hang hope for a better tomorrow. It was completely—boringly—normal. Like meeting an online crush after months of e-flirting, the reality didn't live up to the fantasy. It was dull, predictable, and way more attractive in the photos.

Architecturally, the mustard-yellow brick rectangle was plainer than a pack of Trident. The sweaty-pencil-eraser-library-book smell that would undoubtedly morph into a sweaty-pencil-eraser-library-book headache by two o'clock was so typical. And the goofy desk etchings that said BITE ME, LALA!, WEAK FOR WEEKS, and GLUTEN-FREE GEEK paled in comparison to the ones she used to see in Beverly Hills, which had read like TMZ text alerts.

Tired, hungry, and disappointed, Melody felt like a refugee, only slightly more fashion-forward, as she ambled along with the masses in search of food. Dressed in Candace's black skinny jeans (at her sister's insistence), a pink Clash T-shirt, and pink Converse, she was '70s revival in a school that still wore original Woodstock. Her pretty-in-punk outfit seemed unnecessarily harsh amid the flowing skirts and flannel, making her feel like she was at the wrong concert. Even her black hair hung with antiestablishment apathy, thanks to a travel bottle of conditioner that had been incorrectly labeled SHAMPOO.

She hoped the tough girl getup would show the students at Merston that she was nobody's Smellody. Which it must have, because everyone pretty much ignored her all morning. A few average-looking boys eyed her with marked interest. Like she was a slice of cake on a passing dessert cart and worth saving room for. In some instances she even allowed herself to smile back, pretending that they were seeing her for *her*, not some perfectly symmetrical creation designed by her father. That's what she had thought about Jackson—but she had been wrong.

Ever since their conversation at the Riverfront, the sweet guy who wrote his number in red pastel had been physically and technologically MIA. After taping his sketch to her log wall, Melody entered him as "J" on her speed dial. And speed-dial she did! But he never responded. She scrutinized their encounter by reading between the lines, looking underneath words, checking behind gestures…and found no logical explanation.

Perhaps it was the stilted conversation. *But isn't awkwardness something we have in common?* After forty-plus hours of analysis, Melody had reached a conclusion. It must have been her road trip outfit after all.

And then she heard about the ol' "curdy con," a term Candace introduced her to while they rocked on the porch swing, enjoying their last homework-free night of the summer.

"It's a classic sting," she explained after Melody's third text to Jackson went unanswered. "A boy acts all curdy to earn a girl's trust. Once he has it, he gets all Free Birdie and flies the coop for a day or two. This ropes the girl in even more because she's concerned. Soon concern becomes insecurity. And then"—she snapped her fingers—"he appears out of nowhere and surprises her. The girl is so relieved he's not dead and soooo happy he still likes her, she throws herself at him. And once they're in a full-on chest-to-chest hug he becomes..."—she paused for dramatic effect—"the Dirty Birdie! Known in some circles as the Pervy Birdie, or just the Worm."

"He's not *scamming* me," Melody insisted, peeking at her iPhone. But the Free Birdie was silent. Not a single tweet.

"Okay." Candace leaped off the swing. "Just don't be surprised if he's not the guy you think he is." She snapped her fingers and said, "Candace out!" Then she marched into the cabin.

"Thanks for the advice," Melody called, wondering if Jackson was watching her from his bedroom window. If he wasn't, where was he? And if he was, why wasn't he calling?

Melody tried to shrug off the overanalysis and shuffled into the cafeteria with the rest of the students. Everyone scattered to claim a table while the rolling reggae-ish beat of Jack Johnson's song "Hope" spilled from the speakers.

Melody hung back by a sign-up booth for the September Semi Committee (whatever that was), pretending to read about the various volunteer opportunities while assessing the lunchroom politics. She'd assumed she would have seen Jackson by now. It was the first day of school and his mother, Ms. J, *was* a science teacher, after all. But he had obviously skipped out on her too.

The tangy-carcass smell of ketchup and cows (meat loaf?) was more overwhelming than the four different "food zones." Defined by chair color and identified with spirited hand-painted signs, the Peanut-Free Zone was brown; the Gluten-Free Zone was blue; the Lactose-Free Zone was orange; and the Allergy-Free Zone was white. Students carrying color-coordinated trays clamored to mark their territory as if racing for seats at the IMAX 3D opening of *Avatar*. Once their territory had been claimed, they strolled toward the appropriate food station to make their dietitian-approved selections and catch up with friends.

"In Beverly Hills there would be one zone," Melody told the horse-faced brunette manning the September Semi sign-up booth. "Food-Free." She giggled at her own joke.

Horse-face knit her thick brows and began tidying her already tidy stack of sign-up sheets.

Great, Melody thought, inching away from Horse-face. *Maybe they'll come up with a Friend-Free Zone just for me.*

The Jack Johnson song ended and transitioned into something equally nostalgic and groovy by the Dave Matthews Band. It was time for Melody, like the playlist, to change tracks. At least she could cling to Candace, who was seated between two other blonds in the Allergy-Free Zone, reading some hottie's palm.

Melody slid her white tray along the rails, fixing her gaze straight ahead to the last slice of cheese-and-mushroom pizza. A couple standing behind her held hands and peered over her shoulder for a peek at the day's lunch specials. But they didn't sound the least bit interested in meat ravioli or salmon burgers. Instead, they were talking about his latest Twitter update. Which, if Melody overheard correctly, was about a monster sighting in Mount Hood.

"I swear, Bek," said the guy, his voice low and steady. "I want to be the one to catch it."

"What would you do with it?" she asked, sounding genuinely concerned. "Oh, I know! You could hang the head over your bed. And use the arms for coat hooks, the legs for doorjambs, and the butt for a pen holder!"

"No way," he snapped, as if offended. "I'd earn its trust and then make a documentary about the annual migration."

The what?

Melody couldn't feign interest in garlic mashed potatoes for one more second. Curiosity was killing her. With a strained half turn, like the kind used to silence loud talkers in movie theaters, Melody looked.

The boy had dyed black hair with frayed, uneven edges that were cut by either a rusty blade or a vengeful woodpecker. Mischievous denim-blue eyes flickered against his pale skin.

He caught her looking and grinned.

She quickly turned away, taking the image of his green Frankenstein T-shirt, tapered black pants, and black nail polish with her.

"*Brett!*" the girl barked. "I saw that!"

"*What?*" He sounded like Beau when Glory caught him drinking milk from the carton.

"Whatever!" Bek yanked him toward the salad bar. She had on a flowing white dress and peach knit UGG boots. Wardrobe-wise, she was the Beauty to his Beast.

The line inched forward.

"What was that all about?" Melody asked the petite girl standing behind her. Dressed in a thick wool pantsuit and a full palette of makeup, she may have been at the wrong concert too. She was dressed like she would have preferred, instead of a rock band, an elevator pumping Lite FM as she shot to the top floor of a corporate headquarters.

"I think she's jealous," the girl mumbled shyly. She had dainty, symmetrical features that Beau would have appreciated. And long black hair like Melody's—except shinier, of course.

"No." Melody grinned. "I mean, about that whole monster thing. Is that some kind of a local joke?"

"Um, I dunno." The girl shook her head, her mass of thick black hair falling around her face. "I'm new here."

"Me too! My name is Melody." She beamed, offering her right hand.

"Frankie." She gripped firmly and shook back.

A tiny spark of static electricity passed between them. It felt like taking off a sweater in ski country.

"Ouch!" Melody giggled.

"Sorry," Frankie blurted, her fine features contorting regretfully.

Before Melody could tell her it was okay, Frankie took off, leaving her white tray on the rails and the sting of another botched friendship on Melody's palm.

Suddenly, a camera's flash went off in her face. "What the...?" Through a flurry of pulsing white spots, she saw a short girl with tortoiseshell glasses and caramel-colored bangs scampering away.

"Hey," said a familiar male voice.

Slowly, the flash spots began to fade. One by one, like a cheesy special effect, they fell away, and her blurry vision sharpened.

And there he was....

Wearing an untucked white button-down, crisp back-to-school jeans, and brown hiking boots. An unstoppable grin lit his quietly handsome face.

"Jackson!" she trumpeted, and then resisted the urge to hug him. *What if this is a curdy con?*

"Howzit going?"

"Fine, you?"

"I was sick all weekend." He said it like it actually might have been true.

"Too sick to answer your phone?" Melody blurted. So what if she sounded like a possessive freak? He was a possible curdy conner.

"Who's hungry?" called an egg-shaped man with a dark mustache, who was standing behind the counter. He clapped his silver tongs at Melody. "What'rya having?"

"Um." She gazed longingly at the last slice of mushroom pizza. Like a puppy in a pet store making one final plea for adoption, it gazed back. But her pretzel-twisted stomach couldn't do any major digesting right now. "No, thanks."

She made a break for the lighter fare. Jackson followed.

"So, what's the point of speed dial if you don't pick up?" Melody plopped a bunch of grapes and a blueberry muffin on her tray.

"What's the point of picking up if no one calls?" he countered. Still, the corners of his mouth were soft and forgiving, even playful.

"But I *did* call." Melody popped a grape into her mouth before paying. "Like, three times." (It was more like seven, but why make things more embarrassing than they already were?)

Jackson pulled a black flip phone out of his jeans pocket and waved it in front of her face as proof. The screen indicated zero messages. It also showed his phone number. Which happened to end in a 7. Not a 1.

Melody's cheeks burned as she recalled the red thumb smudge—*her* red thumb smudge—by his number on the sketch-pad paper. The one responsible for castrating his 7.

"Oops." She giggled, while paying for her random lunch selection. "I think I know what happened."

Jackson grabbed a bag of Baked! Lays and a can of Sprite. "So, um, you wanna grab seats together? If not I understand...."

"Sure," Melody said, and then proudly followed her first friend (with boyfriend potential) at Merston High toward the Allergy-Free Zone.

Two attractive alternative girls, consumed by their own conversation, tried to squeeze past them. The Shakira-looking one, who had auburn curls and a tray stacked with Kobe beef sliders, made it by Jackson. But the other one, with black bangs and chunky gold highlights, got sandwiched between Melody's shoulder and a blue chair.

"Watch it!" she barked, teetering on her gold wedges.

"Sorry." Melody grabbed the girl's latte-colored arm before she fell. Unfortunately, she couldn't save the lunch. The white plastic tray dropped to the floor with a loud *smack*. Red grapes scattered like pearls on a broken necklace as the divided cafeteria came together for a round of applause.

"Why do people always clap when someone drops something?" Jackson asked, blushing from the sudden attention.

Melody shrugged. The girl, obviously at home in the spotlight, blew kisses to the audience. Dressed in a black-and-turquoise minidress, she had the Olympic figure skater thing down.

When the applause died, she turned to Melody, and her smile came crashing down like the final curtain. "Why don't you watch where you're going?" she huffed.

Melody laughed. It seemed that all high school battles opened with that line.

"Huh?" the girl pressed.

"Actually," Melody countered, gleaning power from her Clash tee, "you squeezed by *me*."

"Untrue!" barked the girl with the sliders. Her statement came out so quickly, it sounded more like a sneeze. "I saw the whole thing, and you banged right into Cleo." The barker wore purple leggings and a black bomber jacket lined in fur the same color as her hair. Not quite what Melody expected from the Beaver State. The Show Me State, maybe.

"It was an accident, Claudine," Jackson explained, obviously trying to keep the peace.

"I've got it." Cleo licked her glossy lips as if tasting the deliciousness of her own idea. She grinned at Melody. "Give me *your* grapes and we'll call it even."

"No way! It was your fault," Melody snapped, surprised by her own courage (and her sudden affinity for grapes). She had spent the last fifteen years giving grapes to bullies. And now she was done.

"Listen, Melodork..." Cleo leaned closer and gritted her teeth.

"How do you know my name?"

Claudine howled with laughter.

"I know everything around here." Cleo opened her arms wide, claiming the cafeteria as her kingdom. Well, maybe it was. Still, Melodork was nobody's peasant.

"I also *know*"—Cleo raised her voice, continuing to perform for her fans in the blue seats—"that if you don't give me those grapes, you'll be eating over there." She pointed to the empty table outside the boys' bathroom. It was spackled in wet toilet paper and crumbled urinal cakes.

In the distance, over Cleo's shoulder, Melody could see Candace laughing with her new friends, floating above the world in her happy Candace bubble, completely unaware of her sister's trauma.

"Well?" Cleo put her hands on her slim hips and tapped her fingers impatiently.

Dizziness overcame Melody. Tunnel vision sharpened her senses and hyper-focused her awareness on Cleo's exotic Egyptian features. *Why do pretty girls always feel so entitled? Why can't she use her beauty for good instead of evil? What would Dad think of the asymmetrical beauty mark to the right of her eye?*

The truth was that Melanie had no clue what to do next. Other people were staring. And Jackson was fidgeting. Was he hoping she'd give in or willing her to fight back? A ringing sound filled her ears.

"Well?" Cleo asked, her periwinkle blue eyes squinting a final warning.

Melody's heart banged against her chest, trying to beat its way out before things got ugly. Still, she managed to squint a comment of her own. "No deal."

Claudine gasped. Jackson tensed. The kids in the blue seats exchanged a round of *oh-no-she-didn't* glances. Melody dug her fingernails into her palms to keep from fainting.

"Fine." Cleo took a step closer.

"Uh-ohhhhh." Claudine twirled an auburn curl with girly anticipation.

Melody's first instinct was to shield her face, which Cleo's ring-clad fists looked primed to punch. But there was nothing her father couldn't fix. So instead she stood strong and steeled herself for the first blow. At least people would know she wasn't afraid.

"You take something of mine? Then I'll take something of yours!" Cleo said.

"I didn't *take* anything of yours," Melody insisted. But it was too late.

Cleo swiped her glossy lips with more gloss, rocked onto the toes of her wedges, and then reached for Jackson and pulled him close. Suddenly, she was kissing him.

"Oh my god!" Melody laughed, unable to process the audacity. She turned to Claudine in desperation. "What is she *doing*?"

Claudine ignored her.

"*Jackson!*" Melody screeched. But he was in a zone all his own: Its color was red, and its lunch trays were shaped like hearts.

Turning left to her right, right to her left, Jackson followed Cleo's lead like they were on *Dancing with the Stars*. For someone so nervous, he seemed oddly at ease. *Do they share a past? A secret? A toothbrush?* Whatever it was, it left Melody feeling like the pathetic outsider all over again.

Maybe Candace was right—you can take the nose out of Smellody, but you can't take Smellody out of the nose.

"Whew!" Cleo gasped, finally releasing Jackson. She was met with another round of applause. But this time she didn't wave. She simply licked her lips, linked arms with Claudine, and sauntered, with the cool swagger of a satisfied cat, toward the open seats in the white section.

"Nice meeting you, *Melodork*," Cleo called over her shoulder, leaving a trail of smashed grapes in her wake.

"What was *that*?" Melody seethed, feeling the heat of a hundred eyeballs.

Jackson removed his glasses. His forehead was coated in sweat. "Is someone a little jealous?" he snickered.

"*What?*" Melody leaned against a blue chair.

Jackson snapped his fingers to the Ke$ha track that had started playing, and began dancing. "I'm just saying," he crossed one leg over the other and spun like he was onstage at the Soul Train Awards. "You don't look good in greeeeen." His voice was suddenly spiked with a shot of late-night radio DJ.

"I am not *jealous*," Melody snapped, wishing Cleo had just totaled her face and been done with it.

"*Stop ta-ta-talking that…Blah blah blah*," Jackson sang with Ke$ha. He flashed thumbs-up to a table full of girls who were singing too.

"I don't get how you could just stand there and let her—"

"Take advantage of me?" He lifted an eyebrow. "Yeah, it was

really awful." He pouted. "So awful, in fact, that I'm gonna go sit with her."

"*Really?*"

Jackson snapped a finger-gun and fired off a round of winks. "Really." He began following the trail of crushed grapes, kicking them aside with Fred Astaire flare.

Melody tossed her tray onto the table behind her. Eating was no longer an option. Her stomach was tied in—

"*Muffin!*" shrieked a girl.

People backed away as if Melody had peed in the pool. The Gluten-Free Zone evacuated immediately, leaving her to stew in her own contamination.

Melody sat. Alone. Surrounded by abandoned quinoa, millet, and amaranth-based starches, she caught a glimpse of her garbled reflection in the side of a dented aluminum napkin holder. Her distorted, peanut-shaped head looked like Edvard Munch's painting *The Scream*. Despite her new face, twisted old Melody is whom she saw. And all the Clash T-shirts, red pastel phone numbers, and nose jobs in the world obviously couldn't change that.

Her gray eyes were hard, her cheeks were gaunt, and the corners of her mouth hung as if pulled down by tiny fishing weights.

"Nice gluten grenade." A girl giggled.

Melody turned toward the stranger. "Huh?"

A freckle-faced girl with dark shoulder-length waves and narrow green eyes sighed. It was the same girl who had suggested the monster-butt pen holder to her boyfriend. "I *said*, nice gluten grenade. You got rid of the blues like a Saks shopping spree. Next time try spilling milk in the orange zone. We call that a dairy dump."

Melody tried to laugh, but it sounded like a moan.

"What's up?" asked the girl. "You seem kinda down for a PT."

"A *what*?" Melody snapped, craving just one second of normalcy.

"PT," echoed the mousy girl who had snapped Melody's picture and made her see spots before *he* showed up.

"What's a PT?" Melody asked, but only because no one else was talking to her and she was tired of being alone.

"Physical threat," Freckles explained. "Everyone is saying you're the prettiest newcomer of the year. And yet..." Her voice trailed off.

"And yet *what*?"

"And yet you're being treated like a total..." She tapped the side of her head. "Ugh. What's the word?"

"Anti-threat," Mousy-bangs answered for her.

"Yes! Perfect word choice." Freckles wiggled her texting thumbs. "Enter that."

Mousy-bangs nodded obediently. She pulled a phone from the side of her green faux crocodile-skin attaché case, slid out the keyboard, and began thumbing.

"What's she writing?" Melody asked.

"Who? Haylee?" asked Freckles, as if there were dozens of girls taking notes on this bizarre conversation. "She's assisting me."

Melody nodded like that was super-interesting and then peered across the cafeteria. *He* was sitting at *her* table, plucking grapes off a fresh bunch and dropping them in *her* mouth. It was 100 percent nauseating.

Freckles's hand appeared under Melody's nose. "I'm Bekka

Madden. Author of *Bek and Better Than Ever: The True Story of One Girl's Return to Popularity After Another Girl Whose Name I Won't Mention—CLEO!—Hit On Brett Then Got Hit by Bekka Then Basically Told the Entire School That Bekka Was Violent and Should Be Avoided at All Costs.*"

"Wow." Melody shook her hand. "Sounds...detailed." She laughed.

"It's gonna be one of those cell phone novels." Haylee snapped her keyboard shut and then dropped it back into her case. "You know, like they have in Japan. Only this will be in English."

"Assumed." Bekka sighed, in a *you-can't-get-good-help-these-days* sort of way. She sat on the table, placed her hands under her butt, and playfully kicked a blue chair with her UGG boots.

Haylee licked her bubblegum-pink lip gloss and adjusted her glasses. "I'm documenting her struggle."

"Cool." Melody nodded, trying to be encouraging.

Something about Bekka and Haylee reminded her of Candace's line between ingenious and insane. Ingenuity inspired their dreams, and insanity gave them courage to pursue them. It was something Melody wanted for herself. But she didn't have any inspired dreams worth pursuing now that Jackson had turned out to be a player who bolted when someone easier came along....

"I want to crush her too," Bekka said.

Melody's cheeks burned. Was it that obvious she'd been staring?

"We could team up, you know." Bekka's green eyes bored into Melody's.

Haylee pulled out her phone and began typing again.

"I don't want revenge," Melody insisted, scraping the clear polish off one fingernail. What she wanted was currently feeding grapes to a PT at another table.

"How about a friend?" Bekka's expression warmed Melody like hot cocoa on a rainy Sunday.

"That could work." Melody gathered a handful of over-conditioned black hair and dropped it back between her shoulder blades.

Bekka nodded once at Haylee.

The dutiful assistant pushed aside the abandoned gluten-free lunches, reached inside her attaché, and pulled out a cream-colored sheet of paper. She slapped it down on the table and stepped aside to let Bekka explain.

"Promise you will never flirt with Brett Redding, hook up with Brett Redding, or fail to pummel any girl who *does* hook up with Brett Redding and—"

"Who's Brett Redding?" Melody asked, even though she had a strong hunch it was the wannabe monster documentarian.

"Brett is Bekka's boyfriend." Haylee swayed from side to side dreamily. "They've been together since seventh grade. And they are sickly-ridickly cute together."

"It's true. We are." Bekka grinned with unapologetic glee.

Envy pricked Melody's skin like a mosquito. She didn't want Brett, but unapologetic glee would have been nice.

"Lately he's been checking out PTs when he thinks I'm not looking." Bekka scanned the thinning lunch crowd like a search-light. "What he doesn't realize is—"

"She's always looking," Haylee said, typing.

"I'm always looking." Bekka tapped her temple. She turned

back to Melody. "So, sign the document stating that you won't violate my trust, and I'll give you a lifetime of loyalty in return."

Haylee stood over Melody, clicking a silver-and-red pen — the ballpoint Melody would use, should she choose to accept this offer.

Melody fake-read the document to give the appearance that she wasn't the kind of chump who signs things without reading them, even though she was. Her eyes sped across the words while her mind searched for a reason to walk away from this unusual proposition. But Melody didn't have much experience in the friend-making business. For all she knew, this was how it was done.

"Looks good to me," she stated, grabbing the ballpoint from Haylee's fingers. She signed and dated the document.

"School ID." Haylee stuck out her palm.

"Why?" Melody asked.

"I have to notarize." She pushed her glasses further up her wide nose.

Melody tossed her Merston High ID on the table.

"Nice picture," Haylee mumbled, jotting down the necessary information.

"Thanks," Melody mumbled back, studying her expression in the tiny laminated square. She was glowing like a jack-o'-lantern with a candle inside. Because she had been thinking about *him*. Wondering when they'd run into each other... what it would be like... what he would say... If only Melody could go back in time and tell the dreamy-eyed girl in the laminated square what she knew now...

Haylee returned the ID and then began connecting a digital

camera to a portable printer. Seconds later a photo of Melody, minus the candlelit glow, was being clipped to the corner of the document and filed inside the attaché.

"Congratulations, Melody Carver. Welcome to the fold," Bekka said, pulling her and Haylee in for a group hug. One of them smelled like strawberries.

"There are two rules I'd like to share with you." Bekka squeezed some clear gloss from a tube and dabbed it on her lips. She waited for Haylee's thumbs to make contact with her keyboard. "Number one: Friends come first."

Haylee typed.

Melody nodded. She couldn't agree more.

"And number two." Bekka pinched a grape off a cluster. "Always fight for your man." With that, she drew her arm back like a warrior and whipped a grape across the cafeteria. It bounced off Cleo's chunky blond highlights.

Melody burst out laughing. Bekka launched another missile.

Cleo stood and glared at her opponent. Drawing her arm back, she—

"*Duck!*" Bekka shouted, pulling Haylee and Melody to the floor.

The girls laughed themselves a side stitch as a hailstorm of mayo-coated luncheon meat smacked the table above them.

It wasn't the first time Melody had found herself in the center of a lunchroom drama that afternoon. But it was the first time she enjoyed it.

CHAPTER EIGHT
SPARKS FLY

Frankie ran-walked down the empty hall, her wool-covered thighs chafing. She didn't want to attract attention by sprinting, but she needed to be first in the classroom. It was imperative she find a seat in the back. As far from view as one could possibly be without being marked absent. She didn't need fifteen days of math to know that rumors of a monster sighting plus shocking a girl in the cafeteria equaled trouble.

The bell *bwoop*ed. The halls buzzed with freshly fed normies searching for their fourth-period classrooms. Frankie, mega-paces ahead of the pack, hurried into room 203 for her first geography class. So far, school life hadn't gone as planned, but at least she was living it.

"*No!*" she heard herself say aloud upon entering the classroom. The desks were arranged in a circle! No dark corners. No back rows. No place to hide! Her pre-lunch reapplication of Fierce & Flawless would be her only cover.

"This can't be happening," she mumbled under her breath

while trying to assess which part of the circle would be the least conspicuous. Tiny sparks of electricity shot from her fingertips and sizzled up the metal spine of her pink denim-covered binder. She opted for a seat in front of the windows instead of one facing them, to avoid the sun's revealing rays.

"What's with the circle?" An above-average-looking boy entered the room. He was dressed in a white button-down, jeans, and hiking boots. His swagger seemed more leather than L.L.Bean. What he lacked in style he made up for with sass.

He stood by the door, his head cocked as if admiring art in the Louvre. Only he was admiring Frankie. "I'm thinking we should turn this circle into a heart." He lifted a globe from the shelf and spun it on his finger like a basketball.

Frankie lowered her eyes, wishing she could fire back with something equally flirtatious and cool. *Wanna see me burn your initials in this desk with my finger?* But instead of playing Frankie, she had been cast in the forgettable role of shy normie by the window.

With one hand in his pocket and the other clutching a tiny flip-top pad (because cool guys don't take a lot of notes), he strutted over to Frankie. He took his time as he ambled past the wall of maps and the blackboard, probably so she could admire him. "Is this seat taken?" he asked, running a hand through his floppy brown hair.

Frankie shook her head. Did he really have to sit right next to her?

"I'm D.J.," he said, slouching down in the wooden chair.

"Frankie."

"Pleasure." He extended his hand for a shake. Frankie, afraid of sparking, responded with a smile-nod. D.J. tapped her shoulder with his hovering hand, as if that had been the intention all along.

Bzzzt.

"Well, well." He shook his wrist and looked amused. "Aren't you the little firecracker?"

Crap! Frankie immediately turned away and opened her geography textbook. She began focusing on the introduction to keep herself from hyperventilating. The class began to fill up quickly, and two girls, in mid-conversation, filled the empty seats beside her.

"I swear," said the one with the pink-and-black-striped girly-Goth mini, her lips tight against her teeth like someone embarrassed to talk with new braces. "The caf has nothing good for vegans." She shook two pills from a bottle labeled IRON COMPLEX, and swallowed them without water. Her eyes were smudged with black makeup.

"Why not give the mashed potatoes a burl?" asked her friend, a fair-skinned blond with an Australian accent. Dressed in billowing brown drawstring pants, a tight orange T-shirt, and elbow-length striped knitted gloves, she appeared to have dressed in the dark.

"I loathe garlic," said Vegan, crossing her legs to reveal a pair of pink knee-high lace-up boots that Lady Gaga would go gaga for.

"Not as much as you loathe mirrors, mate," joked the Australian as she pushed back a tangle of rope and bead bracelets, rolled down the gloves, and slathered her dry arms with coconut-scented body lotion.

"Help me," Vegan insisted, lifting her pink-and-black-streaked hair away from her face.

The Australian snapped the cap back on her cream, leaned toward her friend, and began wiping Vegan's cheek with her thumb. "It's not easy," she whispered. "You've got lippy where your blush should be. Looks like you were caught in a paintball bingle."

They burst out laughing.

Frankie returned to her textbook to keep from staring. Even though she wanted to stare forever. Their breezy banter was a comfort of friendship—a comfort Frankie longed to have.

"Faster," murmured the Vegan. "Before he sees me like this!"

There was only one *he* in the class, and *he* was sitting beside Frankie, whispering "Firecracker" to get her attention.

Frankie looked straight ahead and accidentally locked eyes with the ridiculously hot boy entering the room. It was the same one she had been trying not to stare at during lunch. But it was impossible not to. He was wearing a picture of her grandfather Victor right there on his T-shirt. He was either a RAD or a RAD lover. Either way, it meant she had a chance.

"'Scuse me, Sheila," said the Australian, waking Frankie from her daydream.

"Actually, it's Frankie," she said politely.

Vegan leaned forward. "Blue calls everyone Sheila when she doesn't know their name. It's an Australian thing."

"Right-o," Blue said with a sweet smile. "Anyway, Frankie, it looks like you're pretty into makeup, and I was wondering if my Lala could borrow some."

"Um, sure," Frankie dug into her GREEN IS THE NEW BLACK

tote and pulled out the gold Fierce & Flawless makeup case marked EYELINER. "Take your pick."

"This is *all* eyeliner?" Lala gasped, lips pressed against her teeth.

Frankie nodded, unsure whether she should feel pride or shame.

Melody, the girl she'd shocked in the cafeteria, hurried in after the teacher and grabbed the seat across from Frankie. She smiled cordially. Or was that normie for *I'm onto you?*

Frankie pulled her turtleneck up to keep her sparking bolts from giving her away.

The teacher, a woman with short curly blond hair and a turquoise sweater set, clapped. "Let's begin!" She drew a big circle on the blackboard and tapped her long stick of chalk in the center. "This is our world. It's round, just like the configuration of your desks. And I intend to show you how—" The chalk snapped in half and shot across the room.

"Ahhhh!" The possible RAD gripped the side of his neck and fell off his chair. "I've been hit!"

Everyone laughed. Frankie leaned forward, concerned.

"That's enough, Brett." The humorless teacher sighed as she picked the errant piece of chalk off the ground.

Brett. Brett and Frankie. Brankie. Frett. Frankie B., just like the jeans.... No matter how she said it, they sounded great together.

He crawled back onto his chair and locked eyes with Frankie, making her spark more. For an instant it felt as though his performance was just for her.

Over the span of the next forty-five minutes, she managed to glean that Lala had a crush on D.J. That D.J. had a crush on his "Firecracker." That Lala could *have* D.J. because, while he was cute, he didn't have Brett's mysterious edge. And that Melody's RAD-ar must have been beeping because she could not stop staring at D.J., who would *not* stop trying to get rezapped. It took a tremendous amount of physical control—which felt like trying not to think, which felt like not being able to breathe, which felt like being dead—for Frankie not to light up like Vegas.

When the bell *bwoop*ed, she bolted from her seat and raced to the girls' bathroom. Lala and Blue called after her, but she ignored them. Frankie didn't know if she had enough willpower to hold back any more sparks.

She burst into the bathroom, locked herself in the first stall, and let it rip. She was thankful that the bathroom was empty, because energy—charged by making eye contact with Brett, being poked at by D.J., and being stared down by Melody—flew from her fingers in a powerful bout. She flushed the toilet several times to cover the sound.

Relieved and drained, she opened the door with an exhausted sigh.

"Sounds like Sheila's got the thunder from down under," Blue said, with a sympathetic smile. She rubbed her flat abs. "I know what that's like, mate."

Lala giggled into her palm.

"Yeah." Frankie washed her hands. Better they think she had to go number three than something so odd that it didn't even have a number.

"You forgot this." Lala waved the Fierce & Flawless makeup case like a flag.

"Oh, thanks." Frankie placed her hand where her heart would be. "I'd be lost without this."

"Why?" Blue twirled a wool-covered finger around one of her blond curls. "You're so pretty. You don't need all that makeup."

Lala nodded in agreement.

"Thanks." Frankie's insides swelled. "So are you guys," she said, meaning it. "It's just that I kind of, uh, have bad skin."

"Same." Blue turned on the faucet and splashed the back of her neck. "Severe dryness."

"You should see all her lotions," Lala said with envy. "Her bedroom looks like Sephora."

"Well, yours looks like the Cashmere Kangaroo," Blue countered, still soaking.

"What's the Cashmere Kangaroo?" Frankie asked.

"I have no idea." Lala giggled. "What *is* the Cashmere Kangaroo?"

"I made it up." Blue burst out laughing. "'Cause I couldn't think of a store that only sold cashmere sweaters."

"She's saying that 'cause I'm always cold." Lala folded her arms over her sweater dress. "Which is why I have a lot of cashmere."

"Are you always cold too?" Frankie asked Blue. "Is that why you wear those gloves?"

"Nah." Blue waved away the notion. "Just dry." She turned to Lala. "Hey, are we going to the spa this weekend?"

"You mean, am I giving you another guest pass?" Lala fired back exuberantly.

"C'mon, luv, that place is so dang exy, I can't afford my own membership. And if I don't get in for a soak soon, my skin will turn to cactus."

"Try a razor," Lala suggested.

"Only if you try a dingo muzzle."

Frankie giggled, tickled by the lyrical friskiness of their banter.

"Hey, we should bring Frankie this week," Lala suggested through tight lips. "I bet some time on the tanning bed would clear up your skin."

"Ace!" Blue exclaimed, scratching her arm. "That'll give you the confidence to nab Brett away from his Sheila."

"*What?*" Frankie clenched her fists to keep from sparking.

"Caught you staring," Blue teased, opening the bathroom door.

"Oops." Frankie pretended to be embarrassed. But all she really felt was joy, to be inducted into their playful game of back-and-forth.

"So, can you make it on Saturday?" Lala asked as they joined the foot traffic in the hall.

"Sure." Frankie nodded graciously. She had no idea what a tanning bed could do for her, but if that's what normie girls did to attract boys like Brett, this Sheila was in.

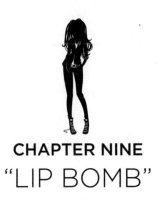

CHAPTER NINE
"LIP BOMB"

On Friday, Bekka greeted Melody with a celebratory high five. "You survived your first week of classes at Merston High." Her freckled cheeks had the same rosy hue as her dusty pink boy-friend cardigan. Paired with dark skinny jeans and knee-high yellow Wellingtons, she was a welcome burst of color on a rainy afternoon.

"I know." Melody hooked a khaki army surplus backpack over her shoulder. "It actually kinda flew."

"You sound surprised," Bekka noted, heading down the crowded corridor.

Haylee followed behind, documenting the conversation. Her orange Sherpa-lined Crocs squeaked as she hurried to keep up the frenzied pace.

"I *am* surprised." Melody zipped her black hoodie as they got closer to the exit. "I was the victim of a kiss-and-run, and that can make for a slow week. But I actually had fun." She smiled, recalling the food fight with Cleo, late-night e-mail marathons with Bekka, and the futile stakeouts during which she and Candace spied on Jackson's house. There was no suspicious activity— or any activity at all.

"Correction," Haylee interrupted. "Technically, the victim would be Jackson, not you."

Melody had already learned to be patient with Haylee and at times even appreciated her passion for accuracy and order. But this was not one of those times.

"How is *he* the victim?" Melody asked in a terse whisper, careful not to give the passing ninth graders another reason to gossip. It was all about lying low after what she and Bekka referred to as the Monday Melodrama, which had quickly morphed into the Monday Melodydrama. And so far she had done a great job. Because whipping an atlas at Jackson's head while he was flirt-touching that Frankie girl in geography would have been very satisfying. And beating him with the Eiffel Tower snow globe while he kissed Cleo in French class would have been *très* cathartic. But she hadn't. Instead, she'd been egglike: a hard shell on the outside, and a runny mess on the inside. So the fact that Haylee could say *he* was the victim seemed more Ludacris than "Word of Mouf."

"Melly is right." Bekka turned to face Haylee. "She's the victim here."

Melody smiled her thanks to Bekka, not sure which felt better: having the support of a new friend or being called by her nickname.

"Melody is *not* the victim," Haylee insisted, her glasses fogging with certainty. "Jackson is." She pointed at the double doors where a cluster of students had gathered to wait for a break in the rain. They chatted in the low hush of funeral directors, obviously deeply saddened by their inability to cross over into the free world. Only two people in the entire group seemed happy: Cleo and the tanned, muscular boy wearing dark sunglasses and a green-and-white-striped ski cap, because they were making out.

"Look!"

"No way!" Melody's hand flew to her mouth.

"See?" Haylee asked, feeling proud. "Jackson got kissed. Now Cleo is moving on. So *he's* the victim of the kiss-and-run."

"She's right," Bekka admitted, sounding disappointed.

"Want me to enter that in the notes?" Haylee asked, rocking back and forth on her tiptoes while tugging the bottom of her fuzzy fuchsia scarf.

"Nah," Bekka said dismissively.

Haylee stopped rocking.

"Who is that guy?" Melody stopped to fake a drink from the water fountain so she could get a better look.

"His name is Deuce," Bekka explained, faking a drink after Melody. "He spends the summers in Greece with his family. He just got back. He's not as cute as Brett, but he's still super cute."

"And super Cleo's," Haylee added. "They're totally exclusive when he's in town."

"Looks like Jackson will be looking for a date to the dance," Bekka noted, peeling masking tape off the September Semi mural that hung above their heads. She balled it up between her fingers and flicked it onto the floor.

"Yeah, well, so will I." Melody pouted, making her way toward the doors. She didn't mind a little rain. At least no one would see her cry.

"Hey!" Bekka lit up. "You should go drop a lip bomb on him, you know, to get back at Cleo for making out with Jackson."

"Ha!" Melody hollered at the absurdity. Everyone turned to look, Cleo and Deuce included. So much for lying low.

"Do it," Bekka whispered.

"No *way*," Melody whispered back. "*You* do it. You want to get back at her just as much as I do."

"Yeah, but you're not committed to anyone. I am."

"Thanks for reminding me." Melody half-smiled.

"Hey, Melodork." Cleo inched closer, the corners of her over-active lips curling with delight. "I've been looking for you."

Projecting Rihanna fabulousness in brown glitter kneesocks, a formfitting denim minidress, and gold wedges, Cleo had the attention of everyone around them. Even Bekka, who glared at her nemesis with a mix of disdain and envy.

"Why?" Melody asked, with egglike composure, even though she felt as if she could crack at any moment.

"I wanted to let you know"—Cleo spritzed her neck with amber-scented perfume, then leaned close and hissed—"you can have that nerdy guy back now. I'm through with him."

The words were spoken into Melody's ear, but she felt them in her stomach.

"Wait." Cleo straightened up. Her blue eyes tracked something in the distance.

Melody peered over her shoulder. It was Jackson. He was walking toward them carrying a fistful of ceramic flowers he must have made in art class. His glasses hid the expression in his eyes, but Melody could tell by his tentative gait that he was nervous.

"I may be through with him"—Cleo licked her glossy lips—

76

"but he's obviously not through with me." She pouted and sighed. "Poor guy. Look at those pathetic flowers. No girl is going to choose geek when she could have Greek." Cleo mussed Melody's black hair condescendingly. "Except you." She laughed.

Melody looked directly into Cleo's eyes, her heart beating like a battle drum. But Cleo glared back, refusing to back down from whatever it was they were *really* fighting about. *Territory? PT status? Grapes?* Melody told herself that Cleo was a typical bully just testing the new girl. That she should fight her hate with love. Be the bigger person. Walk away. Stay out of trouble. Lie low. Check her ego at the door. Move past it. Get over it. Sleep on it....

And then Cleo winked at Jackson. Not because she liked him, but because she didn't and Melody did.

Crack.

Without warning, Melody's hard shell broke, and her insides were exposed. But instead of collapsing into a sticky mess, she pushed past Cleo, marched up to Deuce, and pulled him toward her. Somehow she found his lips and...

A collective gasp was the only way Melody knew she was not imagining this. Then there was the part where Deuce's pre-glossed lips softened and began kissing her back. And the part where she could smell his leather jacket. And the part where she opened her eyes for a second and saw her reflection in his sunglasses, along with the reflection of half the school standing behind her...

She was really doing this!

Melody pulled away. Instead of thinking about the high fives she would get from Haylee and Bekka, the respect she would get from her classmates, the wonderful humiliation she might have caused Cleo, or even the damage she might have done to herself, all she could think about was Jackson—and wonder whether he cared.

"Woooo-hoooooooooo!" Bekka and Haylee hollered. It was the first time anyone had cheered for her since she stopped singing.

"Sorry," Melody mumbled softly to Deuce.

"I'm not," he mumbled back with a grin.

"Not bad." Cleo applauded the impromptu performance with slow measured claps. "Next time try not to look so constipated." She did her best to sound unaffected, but moist eyes gave her away.

Melody didn't respond. Instead, she searched Cleo's hands for Jackson's ceramic flowers. But the ring-clad fists held nothing except anger. Jackson was gone.

"Are you okay?" Cleo asked Deuce as if he'd been attacked. Her expression was strained. She was fighting her bucking cool with the determination of a bull rider.

"I-I don't know." Appearing dazed, Deuce rubbed his tanned forehead. "What happened?" he asked, leaning against the wall as though he might pass out.

He could kiss, but he couldn't act.

"Can we have some room here?" Cleo seethed, forcing the onlookers to disperse and form subclusters.

Melody pushed through the doors in desperate need of air. Instead of a refreshing slap on the cheeks, something that felt more like a damp towel greeted her. A cover of fog pressed down on the front parking lot. A row of headlights at student pickup colored the slick asphalt like a giant highlighter spill, and windshield wipers fought tirelessly against the relentless downpour.

For Melody, however, wet clothes were a nonissue. She was already numb.

"Wait up, superstar," Bekka called, splashing down the steps in her yellow Wellingtons, with Haylee by her side.

Melody stopped suddenly. Not because Bekka wanted her to, but because there was something in the puddle by her soaked black Converse. And it was worth stopping for.

"Uh-oh." Bekka groaned.

Haylee gasped.

Melody had no words.

Everything that needed to be said was carved in narrow script on one of the petals in the smashed ceramic bouquet.

FOR MELODY.

CHAPTER TEN
BOLTS AND ALL

The rain continued into Saturday. Frankie popped open her Astrodome-size, AstroTurf-colored umbrella and hurried into the downpour. Despite her heavy application of Fierce & Flawless Aqua—the waterproof line—daylight shone through the chartreuse canopy and cast a green glow on her hand.

Ha!

She longed to share the irony with the girls in the black Escalade. But that was impossible. They had to believe she was a normie. And her parents, watching from the doorway, were silent reminders of that fact.

She turned to wave. "Bye."

Viktor and Viveka waved back, the worry behind their eyes undermining the smiles on their faces.

"Have fun at the library," Viveka called over a boom of thunder as she tightened her black scarf.

"Thanks," Frankie answered, as a tiny spark of electricity escaped her fingers and scurried up the umbrella pole. It was her first lie. And it felt even worse than she had imagined. Dark. Heavy. Lonely. But if her parents knew she was going to a normie spa with Blue, Lala, and two voltage girls she had seen around school but hadn't met, they would stress about skin exposure. And when Lala mentioned that kids have been lying to their parents for centuries, Frankie decided to give it a try. After all, Vik and Viv wanted her to fit in with the normies. So if this was what normies did...

Blue poked her face out the front passenger-side window. Swirls of blond hair were piled high atop her head like butterscotch soft serve, and her angelic features had been scrubbed clean of makeup. "G'day, Mr. and Mrs. Stein." She waved, revealing a long pair of purple leather gloves.

"Hi, Blue," they called back. They looked instantly relieved.

Frankie grinned. Her parents seemed to know everyone on the street. And soon she would too.

"How're your aunt and uncle liking this rain?" Viktor asked with a trace of familiarity.

"Lovin' it." She opened her mouth and lifted her face to the cloud-covered sky. Frankie envied her freedom and yearned for the day when she could feel a raindrop's kiss on her bare cheek. But until then...

She hurried inside the SUV to avoid a makeup smear, and struggled to close her umbrella without soaking the soft tan leather interior of what smelled like a very expensive amber-scented car.

"Wow." She laid her GREEN IS THE NEW BLACK tote by her feet. "This is one serious pimped-out ride."

"Thanks." Lala smiled, her lips hugging her teeth.

"They bought it off BeyonJay," Blue teased.

"Wouldn't it be Jay-B?" said the dark-haired stranger beside her.

"I like Jayoncé," added the girl next to the window.

They all giggled.

"I'm Frankie." She smiled, mindful not to shake their hands.

"Cleo," said the girl beside her. She had sad eyes that matched her electric-blue off-the-shoulder tee, and the most voltage gold streaks in her hair. Frankie wondered how such an exotic beauty could be so forlorn. How could anything be bad when you looked like her? Were her tiger-striped leggings too tight? "I didn't know Mr. and Mrs. Stein had a daughter."

The girl seated on the other side of Cleo giggled.

"You mean me?" Frankie shifted uncomfortably.

Cleo raised her arched brows and nodded slowly in a *who-else-would-I-be-referring-to?* sort of way.

"Yeah. I've been home schooled my whole life, you know…"

"Hey, Frankie," Blue interjected, "did you meet Claudine?"

Claudine turned away from the window. "Hey," she said, tearing open a bag of organic turkey jerky. Her looks—yellowish-brown eyes, a mess of auburn curls, long manicured fingernails painted bronze—were just as striking as Cleo's but in a more wild, feral way. Her style, however, seemed tamer: all-American with a touch of old-world Hollywood glamour. The fitted black blazer, lilac hoodie, dark skinny jeans, and armful of white plastic bobble bracelets were so J.Crew catalog. However, the tan fur stole peeking out of the top of her blazer was so not. Frankie began sweating at the very sight of it. The heat in Lala's car had been set to Planet Mercury.

83

"It's nice to meet you both." She beamed, folding her arms over her embarrassing peach-colored turtleneck sweater dress. The hideous color matched her makeup, in case of smudges. The prim cut was designed to cover her skin. And the black leggings and over-the-knee flat boots were the result of an hour-long argument with Viveka that, fortunately, Frankie won. Did her mom really expect her to wear peach-colored tights too? Maybe if she was a toddler working the Easter pageant circuit, but this girl wanted friends.

"Everyone ready?" Lala cranked up the volume on the stereo. The Black Eyed Peas blared through the speakers.

"I gotta feeling that tonight's gonna be a good night…"

"Ready!" they shouted.

Lala stepped on the gas and tore out of the Steins' cul-de-sac with a screech.

"I gotta feeling that tonight's gonna be a good, good night…"

The girls fell back in their seats and burst out laughing.

"Oh, your parents are gonna *love* that." Blue bounced to the pulsating beat.

"Whatever." Frankie shrugged. She didn't want to think about her parents. She didn't want to think about green skin or normies or how her bolts were itching from her morning charge. She just wanted to experience a day at the spa with girlfriends. Not through an implanted memory or a Netflix rental. She wanted to breathe it. Live it. Smell it. Feel it. And remember it forever.

"Hey, La." Claudine leaned forward. "Any chance you can turn down the heat? My turkey jerky is melting to gravy back here."

Frankie smiled. It *was* stifling.

"Maybe you should take off your scarf," she suggested, trying to show them she wasn't too shy to jump right in.

"Ahhhhhh," Blue hollered. "No, she *didn't*!"

Everyone burst out laughing except Claudine, who glared at Frankie with her yellowish eyes and growled a soft warning that seemed to say "Watch it, new girl."

"Sorry," Frankie muttered, wishing she could take back whatever it was that Claudine found so offensive. "I was just trying to help." She pinched the wool on her sleeping bag of a sweater. "I'm superhot in this turtleneck, so I was just thinking maybe you were—" Cleo's gold platform wedge slammed into her shin. "Ouch!" She sparked.

Cleo and Claudine exchanged a quick glance.

Frankie quickly sat on her hands to smother the surge. "Why'dja kick me?"

"I was trying to stop you from embarrassing yourself even more," Cleo explained.

"Huh?" Frankie said, leaning forward to rub her throbbing leg.

"Cleo would know." Lala snapped off the stereo.

"What's that supposed to mean?"

"You have a lot of experience with embarrassing yourself, that's all," Lala said, stopping at a red light.

The squeaking windshield wipers were the only sound in the car.

"Care to explain?" Cleo asked, like someone who already understood.

Lala's dark eyes found Cleo in the rearview mirror. "It means you were making out with my crush in public all week."

Frankie wanted to know who they were talking about but

decided it would be best not to ask. There was no telling who she might offend next.

"Do you seriously think I was kissing him for *me*?" Cleo asked, sounding genuinely hurt.

"Um, yeah!" Lala countered.

The light turned green.

"Go." Blue nudged Lala gently.

She stepped lightly on the gas and coasted through the soggy intersection, her dark lashes blinking back tears.

"La, I was doing it for you." Cleo rested a hand on her friend's pink-cashmere-clad shoulder. "He was hanging out with that new girl, *Melodork*, and...well..."

"What?" Lala sniffed. "She's prettier than me?"

"No!" Blue, Claudine, and Cleo shouted. Most people probably would argue that Melody was prettier, letting her classic good looks trump Lala's out-there style. But under Lala's girly-Goth fashion, buried deep behind her dark eyeliner-smudged eyes, lay a hushed confidence. Wise beyond her years, Lala was an old soul with youthful charm. It was an intriguing combination that made Frankie believe anything was possible.

"La, you have so much more to offer than Melodork," Cleo practically spat.

"It's true." Claudine stuck a piece of turkey jerky into her mouth.

"But she was moving in on him," Cleo insisted, "and if someone didn't break them up fast, you would have lost him for the second year in a row."

Frankie eyed Cleo with newfound respect. Beautiful, loyal, and selfless, she gave normies a good name.

"D.J. knows I'm with Deuce," Cleo continued. "He *knows* a kiss from me doesn't mean anything. But Melodork doesn't. And she's—"

"Prettier than me." Lala sighed.

"She's not prettier!" the girls insisted.

"How do you think *I* feel?" Cleo sighed. "Melodork went public on Deuce to pay me back and..." Her voice trailed off.

"He *didn't* like it," Claudine insisted, as if it weren't the first time they'd had this conversation. "He was in shock, that's all."

"I know, I know." Cleo dabbed the corner of her eye with her blue T-shirt and sniffled back everything else she had been trying to keep inside.

"Okay, fine, I believe you." Lala surrendered. "Anyway, it doesn't matter. I'm over him. Did you see how sweaty he was after that kiss? I could practically see my reflection in his forehead."

"You wish," Blue teased.

They all laughed.

Frankie, suddenly feeling like an intruder, looked out the rain-streaked window. She made eye contact with a gaunt, stubble-faced man in a white Kia whose finger was working overtime to liberate something stubborn from his nose. Fortunately, Lala made a left turn before he had a chance to reveal it.

"We're here," she announced, sounding more upbeat. She stopped the SUV under a white awning and gave her keys to the valet.

"I would never do anything to hurt you. We have to stick together," Cleo pulled Lala in for a hug.

"I know." Lala hugged her back. "I'm sorry."

Frankie smiled with her entire body. She felt lucky to be included in their close-knit group, and silently promised never to let them down.

They pushed through the gold-and-glass revolving door and stepped into something that could pass for a normie womb. Dimly lit, cozy, and filled with the sounds of trickling water and muffled voices.

"Hi, Sapphire," Lala whispered sweetly, presenting her membership card to a blissed-out brunette behind the candle-topped desk.

"Good afternoon, miss," Sapphire swiped the card gently before returning it. "Will you be steaming with us today?"

"Yup." Lala opened a book of green guest passes and tore off four. "Blue is going to soak in the salt baths, Cleo is getting the Pamper Package, Claudine needs a wax...."

They giggled.

"Enough!" Claudine barked.

"And this is Frankie," Lala said. "She's going to use the tanning bed."

"Hey." Frankie grinned, her eyes wandering to the jars in the glass case behind Sapphire's head while her hand reached for her wallet.

"Do those creams really work?" she asked, pointing to the line called NoScar.

"Guaranteed to dramatically reduce the visibility of scars in one hundred days," Sapphire said proudly. "Believe it or not, the active ingredient is rodent whiskers."

"How much is it?" Frankie asked, scraping her fingernail along the raised digits of her father's Visa card.

"Eleven hundred for members, thirteen hundred for guests."

"Oh." Frankie dropped the card back into her tote. *Maybe the Glitterati will hook me up.*

"Don't worry," Lala assured her. "The tanning will totally help."

"Cool." Frankie nodded like that was a suitable plan B, even though she highly doubted it.

After punching a few keys on her computer, Sapphire handed Lala several locker keys. *"Namaste,"* she cooed, a brown ponytail flopping over her head as she bowed.

Inside the locker room, women padded across the cream-colored rug, wearing nothing but the spa's plush complimentary robes and the glow of total relaxation. Some were blow-drying their hair while others gossiped about their Pilates instructor's sudden weight gain. But most seemed happy to wander freely and let their normie parts dangle.

Frankie felt the sudden urge to spark. "Are we supposed to walk around *naked*?"

The girls giggled at her naïveté.

"Haven't you ever been to a spa before?" Cleo asked, her eyes no longer flooded with sadness. Instead, they glinted with keen suspicion.

"No," Frankie admitted.

Cleo raised a curious eyebrow. Frankie chose to ignore it.

"Here," Lala said, handing each girl a key. With a single twist, Frankie's dark-wood locker popped open. Inside were the plush robe and padded slippers she was expected to wear during her visit. "Voltage!" she said, marveling at her discovery. But her relief quickly changed to panic once she took a closer look at the robe.

Hitting just below the knees and missing a turtleneck, it was sure to expose her seams and bolts, something not even Fierce & Flawless could conceal.

Cleo and Lala began to undress while casually talking about the September Semi.

"Obviously, I'm going with Deuce," Cleo said, all traces of Melody insecurity gone.

"I need to find a new crush," Lala cinched her robe and then rubbed her arms to stave off a chill that didn't exist. "Who do you want to go with?" she asked Claudine.

"Moot." Claudine grabbed her robe and padded toward the bathroom stalls. "Like my brothers would ever let a guy take me to a dance," she called over her shoulder.

"They're really overprotective," Blue explained, spraying the complimentary Evian facial mist inside her black rain boots. "I'm completely crushless, so I'll be Claudine's date." She shrugged, like it was no biggie. "What about you, Frankie?"

"I dunno." She sat on the bench and hugged the robe like a pillow. "I still think that Brett guy is cute."

"Good luck getting him away from Bekka." Cleo gathered her silky black hair into a high pony and pinky-dabbed Smith's Rosebud Salve on her lips. "She's got more grip than Krazy Glue."

"More cling than Saran wrap," Lala added.

"More hold than Final Net." Cleo giggled.

"More possession than *The Exorcist*," Lala managed.

"More clench than butt cheeks," Blue chimed in.

"More competition than *American Idol*." Frankie stuck out her chest and showed them her diva booty roll.

The girls burst out laughing.

"Nice!" Blue lifted her purple-gloved hand.

Frankie slapped it without a single spark.

"I hate to be a downer...." Claudine shuffled back into the conversation wearing her slippers and robe. Yet for some reason she refused to take off her fur stole—something Frankie wouldn't dare comment on again. "But that girl will destroy you if she catches you with Brett."

"I'm not worried." Frankie tossed back her hair. "I've seen all the teen movies, and the nice girl always gets the boy in the end."

"Yeah, but this is real life." Cleo rubbed the side of her face as though she'd been struck by a phantom blow. "And Bekka doesn't mess around. She jaw-decked me after I kissed Brett during a game of spin the bottle."

"*Really?* Isn't that the whole point of the game?" Frankie asked, secretly wondering what it was like to kiss Brett's RAD-loving lips.

"Yeah, well, the bottle didn't exactly land on Cleo," Lala explained with a wry smirk.

"And Deuce *was* in Greece...." A wicked flicker danced behind Cleo's eyes. "But still...she didn't have to *punch*!"

"Ugh!" Blue scratched her shins. "I have to soak before I hit bone." She fastened her robe and then made a break for the frosted-glass door marked SALT BATHS. Her gloves and rain boots were still on.

Two women dressed in pink uniforms appeared, clipboards in hand.

"Ms. Wolf," said an older blond, smiling, "I'm Theresa, your wax technician."

"Wait? Where's Anya?" Claudine asked, her yellow eyes darting in panic.

"Wellness seminar," Theresa stated, and then splayed an arm, pointing Claudine down the hall toward the treatment rooms. "Shall we?"

Claudine stood, pinched the top of her robe closed, and followed Theresa down the hall. She looked back at the girls and crossed her eyes, letting them know she was less than pleased with the sub.

"Ready, Cleo?" asked the second woman, over the drone of hair dryers. She held out a bowl of red grapes.

"Thanks, Blythe." Cleo accepted the grapes and then waved good-bye, lowering one finger at a time.

"The tanning bed is in room thirteen," Lala explained, her teeth chattering. "Read the operating instructions before you get naked. It's cold in there. I'm going to steam."

"Okay, thanks." Frankie smiled, grateful that she didn't have to undress in front of them.

Room 13 smelled like normie sweat and sunshine. It was absolutely toasty inside. *Maybe Lala has circulation issues*, Frankie thought, locking the door and fortifying it with a chair. A curved bed that looked more like the love child of a Hummer and a coffin lay waiting. A small vinyl pillow and a folded towel rested neatly on its sanitized glass mattress.

After reading the instructions, Frankie's suspicions were confirmed. Fifteen minutes on the bed would not solve her problems. It wouldn't make Brett like her. And it would not turn her skin white. Nothing would. But it might bring back that electrifying buzz she'd felt while standing with her bare face beneath the sun at Mount Hood High. That charge from the sun was bigger than anything Carmen Electra ever gave her, and its warmth had hummed all the way down to her ankle seams. And if it wasn't all that, so what? At the very least, her fifteen minutes would be something to add to her small but growing collection of real-life experiences.

Giddy with anticipation and grateful for the privacy, Frankie wiggled out of her turtleneck sweater and whipped it into the corner. Minutes later she was resting her head on the vinyl pillow wearing nothing but the seams and bolts her dad had given her, a coat of Fierce & Flawless, and silver protective eye stickers.

Feeling for the wall behind her head, Frankie located the power button and pressed. With a single amplified *clack*, rows of fluorescent bulbs snapped on. She lowered the roof and wiggled her way to ultimate comfort.

Ahhhhhhhhhh. There it is…the buzz… just as she remembered.

Unlike a home charge, which streamed the electricity through her bolts, this penetrated every inch of her skin. It was the difference between a drink of water and a bath. And it felt absolutely voltage.

Visions of herself in a string bikini, frolicking on a secluded beach with Brett, filled Frankie's imagination. Warmed by nature's heat lamp, her bolts, seams, and rock-solid green abs would wake his inner poet and inspire him to write. Fine sand would warm the spaces between her toes, and their late-night bonfire would crackle and spark in the darkness. They would snuggle, share stories of their painful double lives, and find solace in the other's embrace.

Ahhhhhhhh...

These visions seemed so real, so possible, that she could practically smell them. Smoldering marshmallows left to blacken while their lips expressed love...smoke pirouetting all around them... the burned-cardboard stink of singed hair...

AHHHHHHHHHH!

"Oh no!" Frankie shot upright, whacking her forehead on the glass roof of the tanning bed. She ripped the stickers off her eyes and saw ribbons of smoke rising from her ankle seams. Her bolts were spraying like sparklers.

"Oh no oh no ohnoohnoohnoohnohnohnohnoooo!" Shaky and confused, she pressed the yellow button on the wall, hoping to cut the power, but that just tacked on another ten minutes to her session.

"Stop! Stop!" She smacked the smoldering seams, but panic made her spark even more.

Frankie reached for the black cord in the wall and yanked. But it held tight. She tried again. And again...

Sparks were shooting everywhere. All of a sudden, a flash of electricity shot from her hand, snaked along the cord, and slithered into the outlet.

Pop!

The room went completely black.

"What happened to the lights?" someone shouted in panic from the room next door. It sounded like Cleo.

Several other voices—some amused, most agitated—fused in a chorus of dismay and mild anxiety. Through the crack under the door, Frankie saw flickering candlelight, and she heard hurried footsteps pass by the room.

"Is something burning?" asked a concerned female.

Paying little mind to her stinky seams, Frankie speed-dressed, then slipped into the dark hallway. After following the red EXIT signs to the back door, she raced out into the pouring rain without a single word to anyone.

Outside, steam billowed around her sparking body like some cheap dry-ice effect in a B horror movie. But she refused to cry. After all, she'd gotten her day at the spa. She breathed it. Lived it. Smelled it. Felt it. And (unfortunately) she would remember it forever.

Frankie's cell rang. It was Blue. Then Lala. Then Blue. Then Lala. She let the calls go to voice mail.

After a soaking six-mile walk, Frankie turned onto Radcliffe Way. Her limbs were loose and her energy, zapped. Still, she refused to cry. She had to save her stamina for the inevitable lecture she would get from her parents. *You went where? You did what to their power? What if someone saw you? What were you thinking, walking so far on such a low charge? Do you know how dangerous that was? Not just for you but for all the RADs! Frankie, how many times…*

Just then a green BMW SUV sped by, its tires parting a puddle that rose up like the Red Sea. One wave smacked the passenger-side door. The other wave drenched Frankie.

This time she cried.

CHAPTER ELEVEN
"EYES ON THE PRIZE, ESPECIALLY WITH GUYS"

"Are you sure you don't want to camp with us?" Glory shouted over the deafening moan of an inflating air mattress. "It stopped raining. And the fresh air will be good for your lungs."

They were in the partially unpacked living room, watching through the sliding glass doors as Beau struggled to assemble a khaki GigaTent.

"Positive." Melody snickered at the thought. Who were her parents kidding? Cashmere jammies, an eight-person sleeping dome, Frette sheets over an AeroBed, takeout Korean beef skewers, a carafe of mojitos, and a projector loaded with season one of *Lost* did not qualify as camping. Why not wrap her mouth around the exhaust pipe on a Los Angeles city bus and call it an inhaler?

Besides, she had plans. As soon as Candace left on her third date of the week, Melody would sneak into her room with a bag of kettle corn and watch her favorite show, *The Biggest Loser*. Only it wasn't on TV, and it wasn't about weight loss. It was about a girl named Melody whose crush on an unpredictable curdy finds her alone on a Saturday night staring at his bedroom window. And it was on its third night of repeats.

"Candace out," her sister announced, appearing before them in an ultra-sheer, off-the-shoulder minidress in a purple, blue, and white tie-dyed print. The silver ankle booties made it perfectly clear, should anyone wonder, that she was *sooo* not from around here.

"How's the hair?" she asked, palming her beachy blond curls. "Too sexy?"

"Do you even hear yourself?" Melody asked, surprised into a giggle.

"I'm going out with Jason. He's a total B-lister," Candace explained, reglossing her lips. "I don't want to give him the wrong idea. I just want to make Leo jealous."

"The *dress* will give him the wrong idea," Beau remarked, entering from the backyard. "Not the hair." His steel-gray Prada fleece was flecked with bits of grass. "Now go back upstairs and finish getting dressed."

"Dad!" Candace stomped her bootie. "Are we living in the same house? It's Miami-humid in here. Another layer and I'll die of heatstroke. I didn't even have to use my diffuser." She pulled one of her curls and released it. "Observe." The bounce spoke for itself.

"The furnace guy is coming on Wednesday." Beau wiped his tanned forehead. "Now change or I'm going to stick that GigaTent over your body, and you can make Jason jealous in that."

"*Leo!*" Candace corrected him.

"Why don't you try my emerald-green bubble dress over your

Phi pants?" Glory tested the fullness of the AeroBed with her toe. "It's in the wardrobe box marked YSL."

"I dunno." Candace sighed tentatively. "It calls for black leather booties, and I don't have any."

"Borrow my Miu Mius." Glory blew a wisp of auburn hair away from her green eyes.

"Great idea!" Candace exclaimed as if she hadn't already thought of that. She winked at Melody to show she had.

"You are such a weasel," Melody teased as she followed her sister and collapsed on Candace's Parisian canopy bed. The harshness of the pewter bars was offset by frilly pink sheets and a white satin duvet cover. It was the complete opposite of Melody's bed, which was a black sleep loft from Pottery Barn with a practical desk nook underneath.

"You have to go for what you want in life, Melly," Candace explained, forcing her foot into the stiff leather bootie. "Eyes on the prize, especially with guys." She nodded her head toward Jackson's dimly lit bedroom window.

"Nothing's going on with him," Melody said, hating the way that sounded. *Why is saying it out loud so much harder than thinking it?*

"What about the ceramic flowers?"

"He was making out with Cleo all week. He's probably just using me to make her jealous because Deuce is back." She rolled onto her side. "He's a player, Candi. And I'm tired of being played."

"You give up too easily. You always have." She smoothed her hands over the bubble hem of the green dress and tilted her head to the right. "This works."

Headlights streaked across the log walls of her room. "My B-list chariot awaits."

"Try not to be too sexy," Melody teased.

"Only if you try to be *more* sexy." Candace waved a hand over Melody's gray peace sign sweats, like airport security. "This is not acceptable."

"They're Victoria's Secret," she tried.

"Yeah." Candace spritzed herself with the latest Tom Ford fragrance. "And the secret should never have gotten out."

She mussed Melody's hair. "You should think about getting out for a while. If the boredom doesn't get you, the heat will." She snapped. "Candace out." A sultry mist of Black Orchid perfume lingered in her stead.

Melody lay on the canopy bed, tossing a white satin pillow into the air and trying to catch it before it landed on her face. Was this really her new life?

She waited for the sound of Miu Miu boots on the wooden steps and then shimmied into the sheer tie-dyed mini that had been left for dead by the makeup vanity. With Cinderella-like trepidation, she slipped on the silver booties and then hobbled over to the mirror. They pinched her toes but did wonders for her calves. Long and lithe, they had the same delicate elegance as the billowing fabric. The cool blue-and-purple pattern brought life to her gray eyes, like lights on a Christmas tree. She was suddenly something to behold. She began imagining herself onstage singing in this dress. Maybe being pretty wasn't so bad....

Vroooom vrooooom!

If it hadn't been for her ringing iPhone, Melody might have never torn herself away from her own reflection.

She slid her thumb across the screen, putting a sudden end to the motorcycle engine ring tone. "Hey," she answered, rolling her sister's white padded desk chair over to the window.

"What's going on?" Bekka asked. Estelle's song "Freak" was playing in the background.

"Nothing." Melody looked out at the white cottage across the street. Rustic wooden boxes overflowing with wildflowers hung from the ledges. A giant maple in the front yard played mall to the food court of bird feeders tucked away in its branches. Radiating mama's-boy charm, the quaint home didn't befit a womanizer.

"What are you doing?" Melody wondered. "I thought you and Brett were hanging out. What happened to sneaking into the new *Saw* at the Cineplex?"

Estelle was replaced by the *click clack click clack click clack* of fingers on a keyboard.

"My parents want me to stay home because of the whole monster thing." She smacked something solid. "It's so lame. I waited all week to hang out with him, and now..." She smacked the solid thing again. "We were only going to the movies. What do they think? We'll be attacked by the Wolfman? Ghostface? Oh, no, wait. What about the Piranha?"

Click clack click clack click clack...

"Why don't you ask Brett to come over?" Melody asked, squinting to determine whether the flicker behind Jackson's blinds was a sign of activity or wishful thinking.

"I did. He won't." Her tone shifted from anger to disappointment. "He has to see it opening weekend. So he's going with Heath...or so he says."

Click clack click clack click clack...

Jackson's bedroom light shut off. Melody's show was canceled.

"Explain this whole monster thing," she said, finally showing some interest. People at school had been talking about an incident at Mount Hood High, but she hadn't given it any serious attention. After all, they'd been talking about *monsters.* Besides, nothing could be scarier than the girls at Beverly Hills High, so why panic? But parents keeping kids indoors made it sort of seem real...almost. "Is it actually legit?"

"My parents seem to think so." Bekka groaned.

"Mine too," said a familiar voice.

"Haylee?"

"Hey, Melody."

"When did you get on the phone?" Melody asked, wondering if she missed that detail while peering into Jackson's bedroom.

"She's on all my calls," Bekka explained. "Transcribing for the book."

"Oh." Melody bit her thumbnail, finally realizing that the background noise was Haylee's typing. She wasn't sure how she felt about the invasion. "Anyway, where were we?"

Click clack click clack click clack...

"Monsters," Haylee stated.

"Right, thanks." Bekka inhaled sharply. "There are all kinds of rumors floating around, but I go with Brett's story because he is super into this stuff."

Click clack click clack click clack...

"He says that there are families of monsters that live in Hells Canyon, about two hundred miles from here. They drink and bathe in Snake River and feed in the Seven Devils Mountains. In the summer the canyon gets so hot they migrate west to the ocean, traveling only at night or on super-foggy mornings."

All of a sudden Jackson passed in front of his window. The surprise sighting gave Melody a chill. She had never actually seen him in his room before. She turned off the light in Candace's room so that he couldn't see in, and feigned interest in Bekka's lesson in local folklore.

"Really?"

Click clack click clack click clack…

"That's what Brett says," Bekka explained. "Then when fall comes and things cool off, they go back. So it makes perfect sense that there was a sighting, because it's peak migration season."

"I shouldn't have kissed Deuce," Melody said sulkily, tired of the hokey monster talk. "It only made things worse."

"What things?" Bekka asked. "You and Jackson weren't in a relationship."

"Harsh." Melody giggled. Her new friend was right. This stalking-and-sulking routine was getting stale. It was the anti–fresh start.

"It's true," Haylee confirmed Bekka's allegation.

"I know." Melody leaned her forehead against the cool window. It was the closest thing to a splash of cold water she could find. "I totally fell for the shy-artist thing. He's not even that cute."

Click clack click clack click clack…

"Thanks a lot," said a boy's voice.

Melody jumped. "Ahhhhhhhh!" She whip-turned to face the thin silhouette in Candace's darkened doorway. Adrenaline revved her heart like an outboard motor.

"Melody, are you okay? Answer me!" Bekka shouted into the phone. "Is it the monster?"

Click clack click clack click clack...

"No. I'm fine." Melody placed a hand over her booming chest. "It's just Jackson. I'll call you back."

Click cl—

She hung up and tossed the phone on Candace's bed.

"Was that Deuce?" he asked.

Basking in the warmth of his jealousy, Melody decided to let him think it was. "That's irrelevant. What are you doing here?"

"The homeless couple camping in your backyard let me in." He stepped into the darkness.

Melody squinted. "Have you been eavesdropping?"

"Hey," he said, approaching the window. "Is that my room?"

"How would I know?" Melody sounded more defensive than she would have liked. She rolled the chair back to the desk and flicked on the light.

Jackson's hazel eyes illuminated when he saw her. Melody's cheeks burned. She had completely forgotten she was wearing Candace's minidress. Suddenly, she felt very self-conscious. Not because her legs were exposed, but because her experimentation with sexiness was.

"Um, so," he stammered, wiping his slick forehead, "I just came to tell you to stay away from Deuce."

"Why?" Melody grinned vengefully. "Because you're jealous?"

"No." He took off his glasses and rubbed his eyes. "Because he's dangerous."

"Jealous, jealous, jeal-ous," Melody sang like a little girl in a playground. To her surprise, her voice sounded a smidge clearer than usual.

"I'm not jealous, okay? I'm worried." Jackson's upper lip began to bead. "About a fellow human being. Man, is it always so hot in here?" he snapped.

"Yup," Melody said, trying to sound as though she wasn't gutted by his lack of jealousy. "There's a fan in my room," she offered. "But you probably just came to give me that message, so…" She clomped over to Candace's door and held it open for him with all the grace of a giraffe on roller skates. "Have a great night. And thanks again."

Jackson walked out, leaving Melody to feel as if she were falling into a giant crevasse. She lowered her reeling head in her hands.

"Much better!" Jackson called.

He was in her room. Lights on. Fan whirling. Falling down a crevasse feeling—gone!

Jackson had already made himself at home. Sitting on the wooden floor under her black loft bed, knees drawn into his chest, fan blasting on him. He was wearing a navy collared short-sleeved shirt, faded blue jeans, and black Converse (just like hers!). The geek chic of it all smacked of a Marc Jacobs print campaign.

"Interesting," he said, taking in the unpacked boxes.

"It's not so bad." She sat, thinking more of him than her tiny disheveled room.

A short, awkward round of bobble-heading followed.

"So what's with you and Cleo?" Melody blurted, as if her thoughts had been greased with cooking oil.

"Whadda'ya mean?" He closed his eyes and leaned closer to the fan.

"*Seriously?*" Melody's heart revved all over again. "Look, I know you're a player. That's fine. I get it: The best we can hope for is a neighborly rapport, so you might as well be honest with me."

"A *player*?" Jackson practically laughed in her face. "You're the one who was kissing Deuce in the middle of the hall."

Melody stood. How dare he turn this around on her? "We're done."

"*What?* What did I do?"

"I'm not an idiot, Jackson!"

A cyclone of emotions tore through the back of her throat and blew tears to her eyes. She must have uttered that sentence a thousand times. The only variable was the name tacked on the end.

"Then maybe *I* am." He reached for her hand. It felt like the smell of gingerbread cookies on Christmas Eve. "Tell me." He squeezed. "What did I do?"

Melody searched his eyes. They gripped her with same desperation as his hand. "Tell me," he pleaded.

Shaking her head like a Magic 8 Ball, Melody wished the answer would suddenly appear. Was this an extreme form of new-girl hazing, or did he really have no idea what she was talking about?

"Cleo," she said flatly, searching his face for any subtle sign of recognition. But there was none. No clenched jaw. No twitching eyelid. No lick of dry lips. He stared at her with the innocence of a child gazing at his teacher during storytime.

"You kissed her," Melody continued. "A lot."

This time he lowered his head in shame.

"Ah-ha! So you *do* remember!"

He shook his head from side to side. "No, I don't. That's the problem."

"*What?*" Melody sat down beside him and removed her heels. This conversation was going somewhere silver booties didn't belong.

"I have blackouts," he admitted, peeling a loose piece of rubber off the toe of his sneaker. "My mom thinks anxiety may trigger them, but she's not sure."

"What do the doctors say?"

"No one knows for sure."

"Wait, something doesn't make sense." Melody shifted to face him, but it was impossible to sit cross-legged in a micromini. "Hold on," she said, reaching for a box marked COMFY. She lifted out a pair of wrinkled striped pajama bottoms and slipped them on under her dress. "Better." She smiled with relief. "Okay, so how can you kiss people when you're all blacked out?"

"That's a good question." He ran a hand through his floppy layers and sighed. "I wonder if I'm getting worse?"

"Don't worry." Melody touched him gently on the knee. "There are tons of people who can help you."

"I'm more worried about my mom than me," he said. "I'm all she has."

Touched by his selflessness, Melody leaned closer. Her black hair got swept up by the breeze of the fan and whipped the sides of their faces. It was pure Hollywood cheese.

"Relax." She gripped his wrist with mock urgency. "You're not going anywhere. The good people of Salem need us!"

"Then fight I shall!" he fired back, not skipping a beat.

They burst out laughing, letting go of all unnecessary jealousy and welcoming the mystery of their uncertain fate.

"You know that I just kissed Deuce to make you jealous, right?" Melody admitted.

"No, but it worked."

"Yay," Melody squeaked, relieved to hear him say it.

He searched her face, his eyes smiling like he was reading Mad Libs.

"What?"

"Your name," Jackson said. "It suits you."

"Really?" she asked, surprised. Even though she used to sing, she had always thought she should have been named something darker, like Meredith or Helena. "Melody sounds so...chipper, and I'm so...not."

"Yeah, but look at the meaning." He crossed his legs so their knees were touching. "A sequence of single notes that, when combined, make something amazing. And that's you."

Melody giggled nervously, then looked at her calloused bare feet. Candace was right. Would it kill her to get a pedicure every once in a while?

"Thank you," she said, touched by her own shyness. "No one ever put that much thought into my name," she admitted. "Not even my parents. They wanted to name me Melanie, but my mom had some crazy sinus infection while she was giving birth. So when it came time to tell the nurse what to write on the birth certificate, *Melanie* sounded like *Melody*. They didn't catch the mistake until it arrived in the mail three months later. So they decided to go with it."

"Well, it suits you perfectly. It's really *pretty*." He swallowed.

Here it comes....Don't say it, please don't say it, please don't...

"Like you."

"Crap. I was afraid you were going to say that." Melody stood, bracing herself for the inevitable.

"What?" Jackson stood too and followed her to the box marked BEVERLY HELLS.

"Look." She shoved her old school ID under his nose.

Jackson adjusted his glasses and then examined the card. "What?"

"Look how ugly I was until my plastic surgeon father fixed my face!" she shouted, like her frustration was his fault. Which it kind of was. He had told her she was pretty. He'd started it. And it was her job to finish it before he stumbled across the "before" and "after" shots floating around the Internet.

"You weren't ugly at all," he insisted. "You look the exact same."

"Well, then you're not looking close enough," Melody insisted, reaching for the card.

"Wrong." He took the card and looked at it again. "I'm looking closer than you think. And everything I see is perfect."

Wow.

Melody's throat cyclone was building strength. Traveling due south, it was headed straight for her stomach. The heat in the house mingled with the heat in her body, and she was being drawn toward him. "We should probably kiss now," she blurted, shocking herself.

"I agree," he said, stepping toward her. The salty-sweet smell of his skin filled her like kettle corn never could.

Closer...closer...closer...and...

"STAND BACK!" shouted a frantic woman.

Jackson pulled away. "What was that?"

"My homeless mom."

"Can she *see* us?" He lifted the fan to his face.

"I don't think so." Melody hurried to the stairs. "Mom, are you okay?"

"Only if you think getting chased by a giant timber wolf is okay," she called back, "which your father obviously does."

"Glory, I'm telling you, it wasn't a wolf," Beau reasoned.

Melody and Jackson burst out laughing.

"Hey, do you want to go to the September Semi with me?" he asked.

"Totally." Melody smiled. "But only if I can wear this." She struck a pose in her pajama-dress ensemble.

"Perfect." He laughed.

Melody stepped closer....Jackson stepped closer...and...

"THERE IT IS!" Glory screamed.

"*Where?*" Beau chuckled. "I don't see anything."

"Melody! Come down here and tell me if you see anything!" Glory called.

"Coming." Melody rolled her eyes.

She and Jackson hurried down the stairs and said a quick

good-bye. Jackson quietly slipped out the front door while Melody walked to the back of the house.

"Look." Glory pointed at something through the sliding glass doors. "Behind the tent, to the left of the tea service. Do you see anything?"

A reflection of a ragtag girl with matted black hair and unkempt feet, wearing striped pajama bottoms under a tie-dyed dress, stared back.

"Well?" Glory pressed. "Do you?"

"Nope," Melody lied. Because for the first time in her life, the image staring back at her wasn't the least bit scary. It was beautiful.

CHAPTER TWELVE
RIP

Frankie slept like a chicken with its head cut off—her brain and her body were on totally different programs. After five boring hours of restitching, during which Viktor insisted on watching the news, Frankie was safely tucked between a fresh set of electromagnetic blankets with a warm current of power streaming through her bolts. Her brain, however, was running in a panicked frenzy.

Sound bites of the lies she had told Viv and Vik taunted her like a never-ending loop of carnival music.

Viveka: Viktor! There's something wrong with Frankie!

Viktor: What happened? Are you hurt? *(to Viveka)* Is she hurt? *(to Frankie)* Are you okay? Where's your umbrella?

Frankie: I'm okay, just a little cold and tired. *(pause)* Dad, did you know rodent whiskers remove scars?

Viktor: What? *(to Viveka)* Is she hallucinating? *(to Frankie)* Frankie, can you understand me? Do you know where you are?

Frankie: Yes, Dad.

Viktor: Where are the other girls? *(He lifts her and carries her to her metal bed.)*

Frankie: They wanted to go to the movies after the library. I promised you I'd be home. So I left.

Viveka: And they didn't drop you off first? *(She flicks on the massive overhead light, pulls the arm, and positions it over Frankie's body, making it feel like an interrogation.)*

Frankie: Um, they offered, but I didn't want them to be late.

Viktor: You could have called and asked to go with them. We would have said yes, especially if we knew you'd be walking home alone in the rain.

Frankie: It wasn't so bad. But I am kind of tired. Do you mind if I rest?

Viktor: *(He dabs something cold and wet over her stitches.)* Of course not. Go ahead. *(mumbling to Viveka)* They almost look burned.

Viveka: *(mumbling)* Probably just frayed from the wind.

While they assumed, worried, tended, stitched, and listened to the local news, Frankie struggled to get back to that imaginary beach where she and Brett were running freely. She finally arrived—but it was raining.

At some point Frankie must have slept, because she couldn't recall the moment her parents left and turned off the lights. But for the past hour she had been lying in bed listening to the Glitterati burrow beneath sawdust, wondering how to explain her mysterious disappearance to the girls. Lying to her parents about the spa trip was one thing. But how does a human electrical outlet sell the old dead-phone-battery excuse? It would definitely take some practice.

Hooot hooot.

Frankie switched off Carmen Electra and lifted her head.

Hooot hooot.

Either there was an owl in the house or her parents were experimenting with ring tones.

She checked on the Glitterati, expecting them to be scratching at the glass in a fight-or-flight attempt to escape a winged predator. But they had fallen asleep, curled into mini white disco balls.

Hooot hooot.

"Hello?" Viveka said, sounding concerned. Her voice was muffled by the wall. "I understand. . . . We'll be there as fast as we can."

Seconds later, bare feet were slapping across the polished concrete, closet doors were sliding along their tracks, and a toilet flushed.

In movies, late-night calls meant someone had died. Or there'd been a fire at the factory. Or aliens had burned circles in the crops. But this was real life, and Frankie had no idea what had happened.

Her door began to open. The thin band of light from the hallway widened like a Japanese folding fan.

"Frankie?" Viveka whispered, her purple lipstick already on.

"Yeah?" Frankie squinted in the brightness.

"Get dressed. We need to go somewhere."

"*Now?*" Frankie glanced at her phone. "It's four in the morning!"

Viveka zipped the hoodie of her black Juicy tracksuit, her tiny bolts momentarily exposed. "We're leaving in three minutes."

In the background, Viktor was filling two travel mugs with coffee.

Frankie jumped to her feet. The floor was cold. Her new seams felt tight. "It takes me at least a half hour to put my makeup on and—"

"Forget the makeup. Long sleeves and a hood should be fine."

"Where are we going?" Frankie asked, oscillating between fear and excitement.

"I'll explain on the way." Viveka left the room, leaving the door slightly ajar.

The rain had stopped, but the wind was still blowing. Silver moonlight reflected off the slick cul-de-sac pavement, reminding Frankie of a huge bowl of milk. But instead of leaves, hers would be full of Fruity Pebbles.

"Where are we going?" Frankie tried Viktor.

He responded with a yawn as he backed the Volvo out of the garage.

"We have a meeting," Viveka said, a slight hint of worry in her voice.

"At the *university*?"

"A different kind of meeting," Viktor said, eyes fixed on the red taillights of the black Prius ahead. Considering the early hour, a surprising number of cars were heading up Radcliffe Way.

"I wasn't born yesterday, you know. Something's obviously going on," Frankie snapped.

"Frankie." Viveka turned to face her. For a brief moment everything smelled like her gardenia body oil. "Remember we told you there were other people like us in Salem?"

"The RADs?"

"Exactly. When something happens in our community, we get together and discuss it."

"And something happened?" Frankie asked, lowering the window and welcoming the cool night air.

Viveka nodded.

"Was it me?"

Viveka nodded again.

Frankie sparked. "What are they going to do to me?"

"Nothing!" Viveka assured her. "No one knows it was you."

"And no one ever will," Viktor insisted.

"You'll like our get-togethers. While the grown-ups talk, the kids get to mix and mingle with other RADs," Viveka explained.

A tingle filled Frankie's heart space. "I'll get to meet other RADs?"

Brett! Brett! Brett! Brett! Brett!

"Yup." Viveka smiled, turning back to face the road. "Ms. J is a wonderful youth counselor. She leads discussions about the issues you're facing and—"

"Ms. J the science teacher?" Frankie asked.

"Voices down, windows up," Viktor whispered, turning onto Front Street. He pulled up to an empty stretch of curb beside a public park and shut off the engine. "Shhhhhhhh," he hissed, with a finger to his lips.

The Riverfront carousel was directly across the street, its painted horses still and silent, like the rest of Salem. Traffic lights changed from red to green to yellow and then back to red, performing for an audience that never showed. Even the wind had stopped.

What are they waiting for?

Frankie controlled her urge to spark, but it wasn't easy. The beam of a flashlight flickered across the windshield.

"Let's go," Viktor said, stepping out of the SUV.

A man appeared, dressed all in black. Without a word, he took Viktor's keys and drove off with their car.

Too afraid to speak, Frankie looked at her parents on the deserted sidewalk and asked a hundred questions with her eyes.

"He's just parking it for us," Viktor whispered. "Follow me."

He offered his hands and led his girls behind a dense thicket. After a quick scan of his surroundings, he bent down and patted the wet grass.

"Got it," he said, yanking something that looked like a rusty bangle. A hatch opened, and he hurried Frankie and Viveka inside.

"What is this?" Frankie asked, marveling at the underground walkway that snaked before them. Laid with cobblestone and lit by lanterns, it smelled like mud and danger.

"It leads to RIP." Viktor's voice echoed. "RAD Intel Party."

Frankie beamed. "So, it's a party?"

"It can be." Viktor winked at his wife.

Viveka giggled.

The low drone of cars on the road above them vibrated throughout the tunnel. But Frankie didn't spark once. Filled with the hope of seeing Brett, she followed her parents along the cobblestone road with the bounce and promise of a day at Disneyland.

An old wooden door with thick iron hinges greeted them at the end of their brief trek.

"We're here," Viktor whispered.

"Mmmmm, smells like popcorn." Frankie rubbed her belly.

"That's because we're under Mel's popcorn stand," Viveka explained while Viktor searched for his key. "And soon we'll be underneath the carousel."

"Voltage!" Frankie looked up, but all she saw was a mud ceiling and some broken lantern hooks.

"The carousel was built by RADs, you know," Viveka announced with pride. "A very nice Greek couple who used to live on a horse farm, named Mr. and Mrs. Gorgon. I believe their son Deuce is in your grade."

Cleo's boyfriend? Does she know he's a RAD?

"The Gorgons can turn things to stone just by looking at them," Viveka continued. "So one day, Maddy Gorgon hears an uproar in the stable. Turns out one of the groomers' kids was throwing rocks at a nearby beehive and broke it. So when Maddy runs in, she is attacked and starts swatting like mad. Her glasses fall off, she looks at the horses, and just like that" — she snapped her fingers — "they turn to stone.

"The Gorgons spent the next five years painting the horses." Viveka gasped at the sheer magnitude of the project. "And in 1991, Mrs. Gorgon donated them to the city." She giggled. "Oh, you should really hear her tell it. It's so funny."

"I bet." Frankie feigned interest, but her thoughts drifted back to what was behind the door, not above it.

Click.

Viktor opened the door to her new social life.

"Remember," he warned. "In here we're family. But up there"—he pointed at the carousel—"any mention of RIP or its members is forbidden. Even in a RADs-only conversation. And that includes e-mails, texts, and tweets."

"Okay, I get it." Frankie pushed her father inside the round room and did a quick scan for Brett.

Dressed in PJs, kids of all ages were lounging on couches and club chairs, like they were hanging in a friend's basement. Everything in this basement, though, had a casing of smooth white stone. Apparently Mrs. Gorgon had lost her glasses a few more times.

"Voltage!" Frankie gasped. "Look at all the kids!"

"Viktor, Viv!" A woman wearing oversize black Dior sunglasses greeted them with open arms. Her hair was piled high under a seafoam-green Pucci head scarf, and her white linen pantsuit looked surprisingly chic, despite its Labor Day expiration date.

"Maddy Gorgon, meet our daughter, Frankie," Viveka said, beaming.

Maddy clapped her hands over her mouth. "Oh, V, she's just *gorgeous*. Viktor did a wonderful job."

Frankie practically floated up off the cobblestones with delight. She was completely green, and someone thought she was gorgeous! Someone other than her parents!

"Nice to meet you, Mrs. Gorgon." Frankie held out her hand, not the least bit concerned about sparking.

"Call me Maddy," she insisted, "or Mother-in-law." She leaned closer to Frankie's ear and whispered, "If Deuce ever dumps Cleo, I'm calling you." She tapped one of her dark lenses and said, "Wink wink."

Frankie beamed.

"Now if you'll excuse me," Maddy said, becoming grave, "I'm going to borrow your parents." She placed a hand on each of their backs and guided them through the stone doorway.

Once the grown-ups were gone, someone blasted "Bust Your Windows" from the *Glee* sound track, and everyone shot up to dance. From what she could tell, no one else had seams or bolts. But there were a few guys with snakes for hair, a gilled-couple making out by the stone cactus, several swinging tails, and a serpent-skinned girl who resembled the voltage Fendi clutch Frankie had seen in *Vogue*.

"Frankie!" called a familiar female voice.

She turned. "*Lala?* What are you doing here?"

"I'd ask you the same thing, but..." She touched Frankie's green hand. "It's kind of obvious. Besides, I heard a rumor a while ago that your dad was making a kid. I just didn't know she'd be so...voltage."

Frankie delighted at the sound of her own expression.

"So you knew when we went to the spa?"

"I had a feeling. We all did," Lala confessed. "But we're not allowed to talk about RAD stuff out there." She pointed up. "So we've been waiting for the next RIP to confirm."

"Well, consider me confirmed." Frankie smiled brightly, luxuriating in the weightlessness of freedom. "Um...what are *you*?" she blurted, unsure of the polite way to ask, or if there even was one.

Lala took a step back, placed her hands squarely on her hips, and smiled.

Pink-and-black hair...black satin pajamas covered in pink bats...cashmere scarf and gloves...dark eyes...mascara smudges on her forehead...It all looked completely Lala.

"I dunno." Frankie shrugged.

"*Look.*" Lala smiled wider for a photographer who wasn't there.

"Fangs!" Frankie shouted over the music. "You have fangs! That's why you always laugh with your mouth closed."

Lala nodded excitedly.

Frankie was about to gush over how amazing it was they were both RADs, when she heard another familiar voice.

"G'day, mates!" Blue called, spritzing her scaly bare arms with the spa's Evian facial mist. Her forearms were spiked with triangular growths that looked like fins, and her fingers and toes were webbed. "Confirmed?"

Lala lifted Frankie's arm and pointed at her seams.

"Ace!" The fins wiggled with delight. "Welcome to the party!"

"Ahhhhhhh," Cleo yawned, shuffling toward them. Other than her feet, which were clad in a pair of gold platform sandals, and her ring-covered hands, she was totally wrapped in strips of white cloth. The fashion-forward look was so Rihanna at the 2009 American Music Awards. "Does anyone know what's going on? Was there another sighting?"

Lala shrugged.

"Is *he* here?" Cleo asked.

Lala pointed at the three boys seated on a stone carpet in front of them. Deuce appeared to be in a meditative state. Sitting cross-legged and wearing sunglasses, he was playing the flute for the tangle of green snakes slithering on his head.

"Looks like someone's having a RAD hair day," Lala joked.

Cleo giggled into her palm and then turned away from her two-timing, normie-loving boyfriend.

"I can't believe you're here too!" Frankie exclaimed, inhaling a nose full of amber perfume.

"I would say the same thing about you, only I'm not the least bit surprised," Cleo said smugly. "Now pay up."

"Huh?"

"Not you! *Draculaura!*" she snapped, her tired blue eyes smoked to perfection. "I told that vamp you were one of us the first time I laid eyes on you. Now she owes me ten bucks."

"Who's Draculaura?"

"It's my RAD name—my *real* name," Lala said, handing Cleo a ten-dollar bill.

Cleo folded it into the shape of a pyramid and stuffed it down her linen-enhanced cleavage. "Maybe if my family got some royalties from those Brendan Fraser movies or those tacky Cleopatra Halloween costumes, I wouldn't need to take your money."

"You don't need to take my money anyway...but imagine how loaded I'd be from *Twilight*?" Lala said.

"I'd complain too," Blue scratched her scaly arms, "but *Creature from the Black Lagoon* wasn't exactly a bonzer at the box office."

"How did you know I was a RAD?" Frankie asked Cleo, suddenly wondering who else might be onto her.

"I thought I saw you spark in the cafeteria. And then I saw it again in Lala's car."

"That's not the only time I sparked yesterday." Frankie giggled.

"That power outage was *you?*" Blue asked.

Frankie nodded sheepishly.

"Fang-tastic!" Lala clapped.

"Do you have any idea how much I hate the dark?" Cleo asked. "It reminds me of being buried alive."

"I *thought* I heard you screaming."

"My masseuse had to piggyback me outta there," Cleo admitted. "I was scared stiff."

"You mean, you *are* a scared stiff," Lala teased.

The girls burst out laughing.

"It's *so* voltage that you're all RADs," Frankie trilled. "I never would have thought—"

The door slammed. Everyone turned to find a pack of preppy, albeit hairy, boys entering the party, their long fingers clutching supersized McDonald's takeout bags. Without a single word, they sat at the stone picnic table and began devouring their Big Macs.

"Claude!" Cleo shouted at the oldest-looking boy, who had dark, curly hair and was dressed in khakis and a blue blazer. "Where's your sister?"

"In the tunnel crying," he said, chewing fiercely. "She got tagged again."

Cleo and Lala exchanged a sympathetic pout.

"You don't have to howl it to the whole world!" Claudine shouted from the other side of the door.

"Um, you're the one howling, not me," he called, unwrapping another Big Mac and tossing the bun away.

"What am I supposed to do?" Claudine entered, sobbing. "Look what they did to me." She tugged the patch of red fur around her neck.

"What happened?" Cleo patted her arm.

"It was those PETA activists again. They think I'm wearing *fur*."

"You are," Frankie reasoned.

"Yeah." Claudine unbuttoned her navy-blue coat and revealed her amber one. "My own!"

Frankie gasped in horror. Not from the shock of seeing werewolf hair under a sexy nightie as much as from the memory of suggesting Claudine remove her fur. If only she had known!

"Ugh!" the wolf growled. "If the stupid power didn't go out yesterday, I would have gotten my wax, and none of this would have happened."

Frankie sat on the arm of a nearby couch and pretended to pick a loose ankle seam.

"It's okay. You're safe now." Cleo hugged the distraught lycanthrope. "Mummy's here."

Claudine burst out laughing and wiped her wet nose on Cleo's cloth-wrapped shoulder. "That might be the corniest thing I've ever heard."

"No, I think Lala's 'RAD hair day' comment was worse."

"You know"—Lala finger-combed Claudine's tagged tuft while changing the subject—"it's kind of punk rock."

Claudine glared at her. "What's with your forehead?"

"Mascara!" Blue called.

"Surprise, surprise," Cleo teased.

"What?" Lala flashed fang. "I can't see my reflection, okay? At least I'm *trying*," she insisted, sitting on the couch beside Frankie.

"Hey, what's she doing here?" Claudine asked, suddenly noticing the newcomer.

Frankie pointed to her bolts.

"Oh, cool." Claudine sat, unfazed, as if she pierced necks at the mall for a living.

Frankie noticed embroidery on the nightie—it said CLAWDEEN. "Oh," she said, pointing, "is that how you spell your name? It's cool."

Clawdeen looked down. "That's how my parents spell it. But at school it's just easier to go with the normie spelling. Fewer annoying comments."

Ms. J entered and flipped the latch on the wooden door.

What about Brett?

Frankie let out a heavy sigh. He wasn't coming. He wasn't like her. He wasn't an option.

Ms. J shut off the stereo and everyone sat, like in a game of musical chairs. Blue wrapped herself in a plush red robe and joined the girls on the couch.

"Sorry I'm late," Ms. J announced. "Car trouble."

"Yeah, remind me to use that one the next time I'm late for biology," Claude barked.

Everyone chuckled.

"You need to get your license first," she fired back, stepping up to the stone podium that faced the couch klatch.

"Eleven days," Claude announced.

The RADs applauded. He stood and bowed while Frankie studied Ms. J with renewed interest. Woody Allen glasses, a sharp black bob, red lipstick, and a collection of pencil skirts and blouses in varying shades of black made her interesting for a teacher. But as a RAD, she lacked pizzazz.

"What's she in for?" Frankie whispered to Lala.

"She's a normie, but her son is a RAD, only he doesn't know. She thinks not knowing will protect him."

"Is it Brett?" Frankie whispered excitedly.

"Hardly." Lala feigned a swoon.

"Before we get started on today's topic, I'd like to introduce our newest member," Ms. J said. "Frankie Stein."

Frankie stood while everyone applauded. Their smiles so warm, they looked fresh from the oven. She smiled back with her entire body.

"Please introduce yourself to Frankie after the meeting if you haven't already done so. Okay, moving on..." Ms. J said. She flipped through some notes on a yellow legal pad. "As you know, there was a RAD sighting at Mount Hood High last week."

Frankie tugged at her neck seams.

"I'm guessing it was a prank, but the normies are taking it very seriously. Several are staying indoors—"

"Awoooooooooo!" Clawdeen's brothers howled and stomped their loafers.

"Heel!" Ms. J snapped, her bob swinging. "There's already adversity in this world. We need to come from a place of love. Got it?" she yelled.

The boys quieted down immediately.

"My point is, we need to exercise extreme caution until this blows over. Normie interactions should be kept friendly but distant—"

Cleo's hand shot up. "Ms. J? When you say 'distant,' does that mean no kissing Melodork?"

"Is she a normie?"

Cleo nodded.

The teacher removed her glasses and shot Cleo an *are-you-seriously-asking-me-that?* glance. "Then you know the answer."

Deuce stood and faced his girlfriend. "Cleo, you have to let it go!" His snakes hissed in agreement. "I told you she *attacked* me. I had nothing to do with it. I love you and only you."

Cleo's thick (possibly false) lashes fluttered. "I know. I just wanted to hear you say it in front of everyone. Anyway, she doesn't like you. She likes Jackson."

Everyone giggled except Ms. J—and Frankie, who couldn't help wondering why the boys thought Melody was so voltage. Because she sounded like nothing more than a boyfriend stealer.

"Are you through, Cleo?" said Ms. J.

"That depends." She fixed her gaze back on Deuce. "Are *you?*"

Deuce nodded and then blew Cleo a kiss.

Cleo blew one back.

Deuce sat down on the stone carpet. He put on his headphones, and the snakes settled immediately.

Cleo smirked at Ms. J. "*Now* I'm through."

"Nice!" Clawdeen lifted her hand, and the girls high-fived.

"If everyone is through, then I'd like to move on to something a little more...pressing." Ms. J stood and pushed back the puffy sleeves of her black blouse. "It came to my attention during our Friday staff meeting that this year's September Semi is going to have a theme."

Blue raised her webbed hand. "Under the Sea?"

"I'm afraid not, Lagoona Blue," Ms. J said sadly. "In light of the *alleged* monster sighting, they think it would be festive to make it a…a"—she inhaled deeply, then exhaled—"Monster Mash."

The reaction was so explosive, Frankie imagined the carousel popping off its hinges and spiraling down Front Street.

"That's so offensive!"

"Totally cliché!"

"We did that in middle school, and it was lame back then."

"How 'bout we have a *Normie* Mash?"

"We could all dress exactly the same and do absolutely nothing special."

"Yeah, but if we go as normies, we'll have to stay home!"

"And lock the doors."

"And tell each other stories about all the scary monsters."

Frankie started sparking. Not because she found the Monster Mash theme offensive, but because she didn't. Not even a little bit. And saying nothing when you could be right seemed worse than saying something and being wrong.

Frankie's hand shot up. "Um, can I just say one thing?"

Her voice was too soft to get anyone's attention, but her finger fireworks did the trick. Once the kids in the room settled down, so did the sparks. Everyone stared expectantly. But Frankie wasn't afraid. She knew that what she was saying would impress them even more than her light show.

"Um, I kind of think the Monster Mash theme is a good thing."

The murmurs started up again. Cleo kicked her in the shin, just as she had done in the car. But Ms. J clapped twice and returned the floor to Frankie.

"I think normies wanting to dress like us is a compliment," she said. "Isn't imitation the best form of flattery?" Some people nodded, considering Frankie's words. "I mean, who isn't tired of copying *their* style?"

Lala and Blue applauded, the sound of their support charging her like the sun.

"Maybe it's a sign of the times. Maybe normies are ready for a change. Maybe they need us to show them they don't have to be afraid. And maybe the best way to do that is to go to the Monster Mash *without* costumes."

Murmurs rose like abandoned helium balloons. Ms. J lifted her palm.

"What exactly are you suggesting?" she asked.

Frankie tugged at her neck seam. "Um, I guess I'm saying a costume party with a monster theme means we can go as ourselves. Then once everyone is having a good time, we can show the normies that we're not in costume. They'll realize we're harmless, and we'll be able to live freely and openly."

The room was silent.

"I could finally let my hair down," Deuce joked.

"I could take off this ridiculous blazer," Claude said.

"I could smile for pictures," Lala announced.

"Doesn't matter." Cleo grinned. "It's not like you show up on film, anyway."

Lala bared her fangs. Cleo rolled her eyes. Then they both giggled.

"How about we put it to a vote?" Ms. J said. "All in favor of coming out of the casket during the September Semi, raise your hand."

Frankie's arm shot up. Hers was the only one.

"All in favor of staying hidden?"

Everyone else raised an arm. Ms. J raised two.

"Really?" Frankie sat, unable to make eye contact with anyone. Not that they were trying. Disappointment and shame fought inside Frankie for heart-space domination. But total depression came out of nowhere and stole the title.

Why was everyone so afraid? How would things ever change if they didn't take a chance? *Will I ever dance on the beach with Brett?*

"It's settled, then," Ms. J announced. "Forty-three to one—"

"Two," said a boy's voice.

Frankie searched the room for her only supporter but saw no one.

"Over here," said a floating sticker hovering above her. The sticker read HELLO, MY NAME IS BILLY. "Hey. I just wanted to let you know you had my vote."

"Voltage," Frankie said, trying to sound enthused by her invisible brother in arms.

"What are we going to do?" Ms. J shouted.

"Hide with pride!" everyone shouted back.

Everyone but Frankie.

LOST CHAPTER
(WHOSE UNLUCKY NUMBER SHALL GO UNMENTIONED)

CHAPTER FOURTEEN
HIDE AND GO SHRIEK

"Can anyone tell me what an autotroph is?" Ms. J asked her science students, holding up a flash card.

Frankie's Fierce & Flawless–covered hand shot up. Most of her friends were still yawning from the late-night RIP gathering, but she was on fire—in a good way.

"Yes, Frankie?" Ms. J asked.

"An autotroph is something that makes energy directly from the sun."

"Very good." She held up another card. "What about anabiotic?"

Frankie raised her hand again, wishing she had chosen a more forgiving blazer. Tweed was so tight and itchy. At least borrowing Lala's pink cashmere scarf allowed her to lower the collar. But now she was stuck wearing a scarf in class. What next? A whiplash brace? A plastic dog cone? Clawdeen's tagged tuft?

Ms. J scanned the four rows of desks. Her hazel eyes considered each student equally, as if yesterday had never happened.

Meanwhile, Lala, Cleo, Clawdeen, and Blue were just as non-chalant. Dressed in their regular school clothes, doodling in their notebooks, checking for split ends, picking their cuticles...They behaved exactly like every other girl in the class. Bored and normal.

The only person showing any RAD pride was Brett, who sat next to her carving a bikini-clad zombie into his desk. It was definitely a sign. Their beach day was coming.

"Yes, Frankie?" Ms. J said, sounding a little bored herself.

"Anabiotic describes something that is living in a state of sus-pended animation."

"Good." She flipped a card. "And *biotic*?"

"A cyborg!" Brett blurted. "Like Steve Austin on that old TV show *The Six Million Dollar Man*."

"*Who*?" Bekka asked, sounding slightly jealous.

"He was so awesome." Brett perked up. "He could run sixty miles an hour, and his eye was like a zoom lens and—"

"That's *bionic*," Ms. J corrected. Everyone snickered. "I'm asking about bio-*tic*."

Frankie raised her hand, determined to show Brett that she was more than just a pretty face.

"Anyone other than Frankie?" Ms. J sighed.

No one breathed.

"Biotic describes something that's living," Frankie volun-teered, grateful for her parents' biology obsession.

"Good." Ms. J carefully pinched a piece of chalk, mindful of the dusty blackboard ledge and what it might do to her dark attire. "As you know, all things are either—"

Frankie raised her hand again and spoke. "Are the undead anabiotic?"

Lala, Cleo, Clawdeen, and Blue lifted their heads and exchanged a fearful glance.

Ms. J removed her black-framed glasses. "*Excuse* me?"

Frankie couldn't see the logic in being intimidated by someone who was obviously intimidated herself. Raising awareness was the first step in creating change...and getting Brett to notice her.

"What about zombies? Or vampires and phantoms? What are they considered?"

"Yeah!" Brett chimed in. "Zombies are definitely anabiotic."

He smiled at Frankie. She radiated back. Bekka, who was seated on the other side of him, kicked the metal leg of his chair.

Ms. J slammed the chalk back on the ledge. "That's quite enough! I'm talking about real science here. Not some mythical—"

Reeeeewooooo reeeeewooooo reeeeewoooooo...

"On your desks!" Ms. J shouted. She jumped up on her own desk at the front of the room.

No one moved. Instead, all the students looked to their neighbors, wondering if this was some new prank-show trick. How else to explain a deafening siren, their teacher's sudden hysteria, and their confusion?

Reeeeewooooo reeeeewooooo reeeeewoooooo...

"*Now!* This is an emergency drill."

This time they did what they were told.

"Good thing I wore my flats today," Cleo mumbled, admiring the bronze finish on her three-inch gladiator wedges.

The girls giggled, still not knowing what they were being drilled for.

Reeeeewooooo reeeeewooooo reeeeewoooooo . . .

"Silence!" Ms. J snapped.

"Tell that to the siren," Clawdeen barked. Her hands were covering her ears, and her face was contorted in pain. "It's deafening."

Reeeeewooooo reeeeewooooo reeeeewoooooo . . .

"Maybe you have bionic ears," Brett joked, from the top of his desk.

"Or dog senses," Bekka added.

"You would know," Clawdeen hissed. "With all those freckles, you must be half-Dalmatian."

Bekka gasped and then looked to Brett, expecting him to rush to her defense. But he couldn't. He was too busy fighting the urge to laugh.

Reeeeewooooo reeeeewooooo reeeeewoooooo . . .

"Now lift up your chairs and jab them into the air," Ms. J insisted, demonstrating on her own desk. With her black skirt, satin blouse, and paint-the-town-red lips, she could have been in a photo shoot for a new trend called lion-tamer chic. "And make as much noise as you can."

She eyed her students, who were all at various stages of chair lifting and jabbing. Yet not even the most obedient ones could bring themselves to make noise.

"What are we *doing*?" Cleo asked, refusing to lift a heavy chair unless absolutely necessary.

Whooping, shouting, yelping, and stomping echoed through

the empty halls. Clearly, the other classes were more open to this mysterious exercise.

"It's a *drill*," Ms. J repeated, still poking at the air with chair legs.

Reeeeewooooo reeeeewoooooo reeeeewoooooo...

"What kind of drill?" Several voices overlapped.

"A monster drill, okay?"

"A *what*?" Lala asked through tight lips.

"A monster drill," Ms. J lowered the chair, "in case there's a sighting at our school. Principal Weeks thinks it's best to be prepared."

Seriously? Frankie thought her teacher's matter-of-fact attitude was disturbing. *Is she really okay with this?*

"Yeeeeeeah!" Brett began waving his chair around and hollering like a wild warrior.

The other normies did too. Frankie couldn't blame them. They had inherited this fear from their parents. But if they were taught to be afraid, couldn't they be taught not to be?

Lala, Cleo, Blue, and Clawdeen avoided each other's eyes and halfheartedly performed the absurd exercise, just like Ms. J.

More than anything, Frankie wished she could do the same. Cast her beliefs aside for the greater good. Make a mockery of her life instead of celebrating it. Hide with pride...

But it was impossible. Simply thinking about it filled her heart space with bricks. It was one thing for RADs to try to fit in. Acting afraid of *themselves* was quite another. Because fear leads to more fear, as was demonstrated by the horror movies that had started all of this. Until fear was gone, nothing would change.

Reeeeewooooo reeeeewoooooo reeeeewoooooo...

Frankie released her chair. It landed with the sound of blatant refusal. Melody, the other new girl, did the same.

"Pick them up, girls. Let's go!" Ms. J ordered, as if clueless to the mini-rebellion.

"But I'm not afraid," Frankie said without sparking.

Brett stopped roaring and examined Frankie with renewed interest. His black jagged hair poked out in all directions, but his denim-blue eyes were fixed directly on her.

"Well, you *should* be," Ms. J threatened.

"Cool," Brett whispered.

Frankie turned toward him. "Huh?"

He pointed to her neck. A snap of electricity zipped up her spine. All that poking and jabbing had loosened Lala's scarf. Her bolts were sticking out!

"Love the piercings," he whispered, then opened his mouth and flashed his silver tongue stud.

"Cool." Frankie giggled.

Finally, the siren stopped.

"Please take your seats." Principal Weeks's pinched voice came over the PA system. "Rest assured that this was only a drill. But we want to be prepared in the event of another sighting," he said.

Frankie rolled her eyes. If they only knew their dangerous "monster" was acing science.

"Now, guys and ghouls..." He snickered at his lame joke. "The faculty here at Merston High wants to show these colossal creatures that we're not afraid."

Everyone *woo-hoo*ed in agreement.

"So this year's theme for the September Semi is...MONSTER MASH!" He paused, giving the students more time to cheer.

"A gift certificate for a dinner cruise on the *Willamette Queen* will be awarded to the couple with the creepiest costume, so get your tickets before they're all sold owww-ooooooooooooot! Mwwwahh ahhh ahhhh ahhhhhhhh!" He signed off with his best howl-at-the-moon-maniacal-laughter impression. A clap of thunder sound effect followed.

Frankie tugged her seams from embarrassment.

"I'm Frankenstein!" Brett called out.

"I'll be your lovely bride," Bekka gushed. She grabbed his arm and glared at Frankie. Her eagle eyes hadn't missed the moment between them.

More than anything, Frankie wanted to tell them they'd be going as her grandparents. And that the *real* lovely bride's wedding gown was in *her* garage. And that Grammy Frankenstein danced barefoot that night because her shoes rubbed her seams. And that Grandpa made all the men put their suit jackets on the floor so she wouldn't get her feet dirty. But apparently that story was too frightening to share.

Slumped in her chair, Frankie folded her arms across her itchy blazer. She glared at Ms. J, sending invisible rays of shame to the one woman she had hoped would save them from all of this. But Ms. J avoided Frankie's eyes, choosing to sift through a stack of handouts instead.

Bwooop. Bwoooop.

Class was finally over.

"Frankie, please stay behind," Ms. J said, still fussing with her papers.

Instead of wishing her luck, the RADs quickly gathered their books and hurried out, while the normies took their time, exchanging costume ideas and whispering about their ideal dates.

Once the room had emptied, Frankie approached Ms. J's desk.

The teacher removed her glasses and slammed them on the wooden desk. "What do you think you're *doing*? Do you have any idea how risky your behavior is?"

Frankie sparked.

Ms. J exhaled. "Listen," she said, putting her glasses back on, "I know that you're new here. I understand your frustration and your desire to change things. And you're not alone. Every one of your friends has felt it. I have too. And we've all tried. But eventually we each realized that it's much easier, and a lot safer, to go with the flow."

"But—"

"You don't think I want to march up to"—she pointed at the speaker that had broadcast Principal Weeks's announcement—"and tell him that his silly desk dance is unnecessary? Or that it's more humiliating than the YouTube clip of Tom Cruise on *Oprah*?"

"But—"

"Because I do. I want to say all of those things and dozens more." Her jaw tensed. "But I can't. I have a son to protect. And as a single mother I have to put his needs before mine."

"But saying those things would help him," Frankie finally said. "It would change things, and he could have a better life than he has now."

"That's true. The kind of change you're talking about *would* make his life better." Ms. J rested her chin on her elbows. "But that's not the change we'd get. We would have to leave Salem and start all over again somewhere else. Coming out would take us right back to the 1930s, Frankie."

"Um, I think the monster drill has already accomplished that."

"Not even close," Ms. J said. "People lost everything back then; some even lost their lives."

Ms. J gently retied Frankie's pink scarf so it lay snug against her bolts. "Someday things will be different. But for now I need you — we *all* need you — to lie low and play the game." She smiled kindly. "Can you do that?"

Frankie sighed.

"Please?"

"Okay."

"Thank you." Ms. J smiled. Her teeth looked extra white against her matte red lipstick.

Without another word, Frankie gathered her books and left.

Merging with the foot traffic in the hall and hearing how excited everyone was to dress like RADs, she couldn't help thinking that maybe her generation was more open than her parents'. Sure, the girls at Mount Hood High had freaked when they saw her, but that was understandable. They had never seen anyone with mint-green skin before. It was a natural reaction.

But what if they went to her Facebook page? Read her profile? Watched videos of her and the Glitterati dancing to Lady Gaga? Learned about her Brett crush? And friended her friends? Would they react differently? Frankie asked herself these questions over and over again on her way to her second-period class, and each time she arrived at the same conclusion: She had started all of this. And she would end it.

Frankie would keep her promise to Ms. J and play the game. But she would follow her own set of rules.

CHAPTER FIFTEEN
TENDER LOVING SCARE

It was a tomato-soup-and-macaroni kind of night.

Light, the color of muddy snow, was fading. Little by little, as if controlled by a dimmer switch, it begged its pardon from the ravine behind Jackson's house. The fading sky could fool the eye into thinking a twiggy tree was a frail old man.

The rain stopped after school, but it was still "treeing"—a local term for excess water being blown from the leaves. Unfortunately, there wasn't a local term for how bone-chilling it was. According to Brett, these were the ideal conditions for shooting his film *The Monster Hunt Chronicles*. But according to Bekka, he was seven minutes late.

"I hope he's okay." Bekka sat on a fallen tree trunk. She was wrapped with Haylee in one of the ThermaFoil blankets Melody had borrowed from Beau. Made of some kind of heat-trapping silver foil and lined in fleece, they were supposed to warm mountain climbers on the snowiest of summits. But with Jackson snuggling beside her, Melody decided the blanket was redundant.

At first, Melody had tried to decline the offer to be in what she secretly referred to as *The Brett Witch Project*, because she had study plans with Jackson. Although he didn't know it, they had a movie of their own to shoot. It was called *Girl…Interrupted*. And take two of Saturday night's kissing scene was top priority.

But Jackson had been standing by Melody's locker when Bekka asked, and he offered his property as a location. After years of neglect, the ravine was overgrown and wild. And coyotes—or were they wolves?—began howling after dark. Bekka agreed it would be perfect and immediately texted Brett.

"You don't think he's hanging out with that new girl, do you?" Bekka pulled the ThermaFoil so tight that she and Haylee looked like a metallic sushi roll.

"Who?" Melody asked, catching a tropical whiff of her Kai perfume. It was trapped under her ThermaFoil blending with the odor of the oily crayon pastels left on Jackson's hands. Combined, it smelled like first love.

"Frankie Stein," Haylee answered.

"You know, the one with all the makeup?" Bekka said.

"Why would Brett be hanging out with *her*?" Jackson asked, adorably willing to participate in their catty conversation.

"I dunno." Bekka pulled a loose bobby pin from the side of her wavy bob and slid it back in. "But you should have seen her flirting with him in science today. I'm surprised your mom didn't mention it."

Jackson scoffed. "My mom hasn't mentioned much of anything lately. Other than how 'stressed out' she is about something she is too 'stressed out' to discuss."

146

Every time he said "stressed out," Jackson freed his arms of the ThermaFoil to make air quotes.

"Don't do that." Melody giggled, wrapping him back up. "You're letting all the cold air in."

"Sorry." He snuggled back under and smiled at her, longer than a regular boy-buddy would. Even though random wisps of hair had gone AWOL from her already messy ponytail, and she was marinating in her sixth-period gym sweats, Melody felt beautiful in a way that had nothing to do with symmetry.

"I wonder if it had anything to do with that bizarre monster drill," she said with a disbelieving giggle. "I mean, what *was* that?"

"It was a little weird, but hey"—Bekka shrugged—"if it keeps us safe, I'm all for it."

"Safe from what, exactly?" Melody asked, wondering how the primitive chair dance could ward off anything stronger than a fart. "Assuming these monsters really exist, it's not like they've ever hurt anyone, right? Who knows? Maybe they're nice."

"Why are you taking *their* side?" Bekka released her grip on the ThermaFoil and leaned closer to Melody.

She wanted to say, "Being judged on appearances is something I know a lot about, okay, Bekka? The monster's side is my side too." Instead, she shrugged and mumbled, "I dunno, something to do, I guess."

Bekka responded with an illuminated grin. She jumped up so suddenly that Haylee almost toppled onto the wet leaves. "Sorry," she said absently, ripping the blanket off her friend. "You made it!" she called to the flashlight-wielding Brett.

" 'Course I did," Brett called, tromping toward her. His mega-tread hiking boots crunched over dead leaves with monster-truck force. Dressed in a black fedora and a red-and-brown-striped sweater, he was either paying tribute to Freddy Krueger or he *was* Freddy Krueger. Brett's horror homey, Heath, lagged behind, carrying two cameras and the sound gear.

"Hey, Heath." Haylee waved the way most people would clean a window.

"Hey, *Hay*." The pin-thin redhead snickered at his own word-play and then dropped the gear by her feet.

Wearing gold leggings under a satin-and-tulle slip dress, Haylee had obviously dressed up for the occasion. She proved it by choosing to shiver rather than wear her salmon-colored puffy jacket.

Heath, however, had not, opting for ripped baggy jeans and a gigantic black hoodie.

"Cool location, dude." Brett knocked fists with Jackson. "Man, if this was my place, I'd camp out here every night."

"Wouldn't you be scared?" Bekka hurried to his side and enveloped him in the ThermaFoil.

"That's the whole point, baby. I'm addicted to the smell of my own *fear*-omones," Brett said, then kissed her as though they were alone.

Haylee and Heath showed a sudden interest in the cameras. Melody looked away uncomfortably.

Watching a make-out, while wrapped in a blanket with the guy she wanted to make out with, made her feel exposed. Obvious. Transparent. Like her thoughts were flashing before *his* eyes.

Finally Brett attempted to pull away without the consent of

Bekka's lips. The confusion created a sloppy bite-a-juicy-peach sound. Everyone cringed.

"All right, people," Brett announced, scanning the perimeter. "We're losing light. Heath, Jackson, come with me. We need branches so I can jimmy a tripod. I want the big camera locked down for the dismemberment sequence."

Heath collected their gear.

"S-sure. Okay." Jackson wiggled out of the ThermaFoil and followed the other boys into the thick woods.

Haylee raced for her puffy jacket, zipped it up, and joined the others on the tree trunk.

"Jackson is so much cooler than I thought," Bekka whispered.

"He's nice," Melody said casually, trying not to gush.

"So you're buying his whole blackout excuse?" Bekka pressed. "You don't think he *knew* he was hooking up with Cleo?"

Haylee pulled her phone from her pocket and began typing.

"Not everyone is as jealous as you," Melody snapped. Not because she thought Bekka was wrong. She was afraid Bekka might be right. "I believe him."

"Good." Bekka stood, making the fringe on her vintage suede jacket swing. She peered through clearings between the trees and cupped her ear.

"What are you listening to?" Melody asked, her heart revving. "What is it? Do you hear something?"

"No." Bekka sighed, then scurried back to the trunk. "Okay, here's the deal," she whispered, leaning in to her friends. "Brett isn't getting tripod sticks. He's going to try and scare you."

Haylee's thumbs scuttled across her slide-out keyboard.

"Stop typing!" Bekka insisted. "This is serious."

Haylee lifted her head and pushed her glasses up on her nose.

"Why does he want to scare us?" Melody asked.

"He wants genuine reaction shots for his movie. So don't be scared, but act terrified."

The night air turned crisp, illustrating their words with puffs of vapor that resembled conversation bubbles.

"Why are you telling us?" Melody asked, genuinely confused.

Bekka looked at Haylee, allowing her the privilege of answering.

"Friends first."

"Even before Brett?" Melody asked Bekka.

"Always," Bekka said. Her lively freckled face was dead serious.

"Wow," Melody said in surprise. They were really friends. Hearing it helped her feel it. And feeling it was like sinking deeper into a warm bath.

All of a sudden a twig snapped in the distance.

Bekka winked at her friends. They giggled into their palms.

More footsteps crunching over leaves.

Then silence.

"Thank you!" Melody mouthed to her friend. Without the warning she might have pooped her sweats.

Bekka said, "You're welcome," with another wink and then sprang into actress mode. "Do you hear something?" she asked a little too loudly.

"Yeah," Haylee whimpered.

"I'm sure it's just the wind, you guys. Relax," Melody tried.

Another twig snapped.

"Oh my god! I hear it!" Melody blurted, trying not to laugh.

Something that sounded like Darth Vader on a treadmill followed.

"You guys, I'm freaking!" Haylee squealed.

"Brett!" Bekka called.

"Jackson!" Melody shouted.

More silence. And then...

"*Ahhhhhhhhhhhhhhhhhhhhhh!*" Wearing a hockey mask and a bloodstained T-shirt and swinging a plastic machete, Brett charged from the bushes. Heath followed behind, shooting the action with a digital camera.

"*Ahhhhhhhhhhhhhhhhhhhhhh!*" the girls shouted, then jumped into each other's arms.

Brett circled them, brandishing his machete. "Eenie, meenie, miney, mo. What to slice first? A finger or a toe?"

"Help!" Haylee cried. Either she was a gifted actress, or Bekka's warning had failed to sink in.

"Somebody help!" Melody panicked, but only because Haylee was.

"Brett!" Bekka called again.

"Annnnnnd *cut*!" Brett shouted, removing his mask. "We got it."

"That was you?" Melody cried, embarrassed by her own bad acting.

"I thought the camera would have given me away but I guess you wimps were too freaked out to notice." He bumped fists with Heath and then pulled Bekka in for a celebratory hug.

"Jerk!" Haylee shoved Heath playfully.

"Crybaby." He shoved back, then put her in a headlock and knuckled her head.

She laugh-smacked his legs, begging him to stop. But she probably hoped he wouldn't.

"Hey, where's Jackson?" Melody asked.

"Oh, he said he wasn't feeling well," Brett said dismissively.

"Where did he go?"

"I think back up to his house," Brett said, moving in for another bite of juicy peach.

"Be right back," Melody announced to no one in particular. With nothing but a ThermaFoil blanket and the promise of true love's kiss, she hurried off to find Jackson.

"Jackson?" she called, into the thick brush. "Jack-sunnn!"

What if he'd had a blackout? What if he'd had a blackout and fallen? What if he'd had a blackout and fallen on Cleo's lips? Melody slapped poking twigs and sharp-edged leaves aside. Trying not to acknowledge that she was alone in a ravine where there might be a—

"Melody?" she heard him whisper. Or was it the wind?

"Jackson?"

"Up here," he said softly before jumping down.

"Are you okay?" Melody asked. She was wearing the Therma-Foil like a cape around her neck, superhero-style. She tried to look past his lenses to see his eyes, but it was too dark. "You didn't have a blackout or anything, did you?"

"Nope." He shook his head with little-boy cuteness. "But it's nice to know you care." He leaned against the tree behind him and folded his arms across his zippered knit cardigan.

"Of course I care." She stepped a little closer. "So, why did you leave?"

He shrugged as though it should have been obvious. "I didn't want to scare you."

Melody sank deeper into that warm bath. And even though he didn't say anything, she could tell that Jackson was sinking too. It was the safest she had ever felt around anyone who wasn't family. If only she could take this moment, and the feelings that came with it, and seal it off from the rest of the world. So that it could always stay exactly as it was.

Stepping even closer, Melody lifted the ThermaFoil above their heads and let it fall over them, sealing them off for real. And there, surrounded by darkness and heat, rustling leaves and distant howling coyotes, tropical perfume and pastel-scented hands, they kissed...and kissed...and kissed....

CHAPTER SIXTEEN
KISSASTER

…and kissed…and kissed…and kissed.

Sweat glazed their cheeks like doughnuts and salted their lips like pretzels. If it hadn't been for the lack of oxygen, plus Melody's constricting bronchi, she could have stayed in the curdy cocoon with Jackson until graduation. But it was getting harder to breathe, and Melody didn't have her inhaler.

"Air!" she gasped, throwing off the ThermaFoil and giggling at their mutually disheveled states.

"What…happened to…your…glasses?" she panted.

His face was dripping with sweat, and his hazel eyes searched her hungrily. He leaned forward to kiss her again.

"Wait." Melody laughed, pressing her hand against his thumping chest. "I need to catch my breath."

"Here." He leaned closer. "Have mine." His voice sounded lower, more in control.

"What?" Melody giggled. "Where'dja hear that line? Sounds a little Chuck-ish."

"Who's Chuck?" He pulled away, offended.

"From *Gossip Girl*."

"Oh." He dismissed the reference with a wave of his hand. Then he studied her face. "Actually, who are *you*?"

"What?" She giggled again, but something about his expression told her he wasn't joking.

"Seriously, are we in a class together?"

"*Jackson!*" she blurted, despite the tightness in her lungs. "What's wrong with you?"

"Who's *Jackson*?" His expression soured, and he paused. Then his pinched look morphed into a mischievous grin. "Oh, I get it. You're into role-playing."

"Jackson, stop it." Melody took a step away from him. "You're freaking me out."

"Okay, I'm sorry." He gently pulled her close.

Wanting to trust him, Melody found her breath and inhaled deeply. He smelled different, like vitamins. Or was that the stench of reality after the love had gone?

"So if I'm *Jackson*, who are you?"

"Ew!" She pushed him away. "Enough!"

"Wait." He took a step back. "I don't get it. Are you into this or not? 'Cause I'm up for anything. I just want to know."

Melody's stomach roiled. Was this another one of Brett's jokes? Was Jackson part of his crew? Had Bekka set her up and lured her into their twisted circle so they could capture a realistic heartbreak scene? She quickly searched the bushes for a hidden camera.

"I bet some music would help," Jackson said. "Maybe we

should head back to your place." He offered his hand. The pastel stains were gone.

"No, thanks," Melody said with a sniff. She grabbed her ThermaFoil off the wet ground and wrapped it around her like a sympathetic hug.

"So it's like that, huh?" He pulled back his hand and ran it through his sweaty hair. "It's okay. I'm kind of stuck on someone else, anyway. And she's a real firecracker!"

Melody opened her mouth. But nothing came out. Even her voice was lost.

"Bye," she managed, then hurried for home, her trembling body desperate to release the hurricane of tears gaining force behind her eyes. But she fought the surge, refusing to give Jackson any more of whatever was left inside her to give.

As she darted across Radcliffe Way, the first few drops eked their way out and rolled down her cheeks—the calm before the storm. Still, Melody managed to text Bekka a word of advice before her vision blurred completely.

MELODY: If Brett wants to find real monsters he should date guys. ☹

She hit SEND.
And the dam broke.

CHAPTER SEVENTEEN
"PUT THE *BOY* IN *BOYCOTT*"

"Frankie, dear, pass the asparagus to our guests, please," Viveka asked, with a hint of Madonna's fake English accent. But Frankie wasn't surprised. Everything about her parents' little dinner party had been contrived. Right down to the relaxed smiles on their faces.

The truth was, if she had a horse, Viveka would have ridden through the kitchen that morning shouting, "The normies are coming! The normies are coming!" Instead, she triple-checked everyone's makeup, wrapped their turtlenecks with scarves and closed the door to the Fab.

"Tonight is very important for our family," she had warned earlier, as Frankie helped her set five places at a table that usually sat three. "The new dean may give your father a lot of research money, so we need to make a good impression."

First Ms. J, and now her mother; Frankie was tired of being told how to behave around normies. "Should I set places for the Glitterati?" she asked, unable to squelch her frustration.

Viveka set the last plate down with an audible *clink*. "Excuse me?"

"Won't they be the ones affected if Daddy gets this money?" Frankie folded a steel-gray cloth napkin and set it in place. "You know, since he'll be experimenting on them."

"Actually, it's wounded veterans and people in hospitals waiting for organ transplants who will be affected by Dean Mathis's money."

"You mean *normies* in hospitals, right?" Frankie pressed.

"Everyone," insisted Viveka. She lowered her violet eyes. "Eventually."

The timer went off in the kitchen.

Viveka hurried to remove the roast from the oven. "Finally!" She sighed, pulling her dark hair to one side and examining the sizzling beef. "Perfect. Third one's a charm."

"You know"—Viveka returned to the table with two more crystal glasses and a new spring in her stride—"if this goes according to plan, one day your dad won't need seams to put people back together. His artificial body parts will attach to the patients' existing tissue and regenerate."

"Because seams are ugly, right?" Frankie's eyes pooled.

"No, Frankie, that's not what I'm saying." Viveka hurried to her daughter's side.

"Well, that's what you said!" Frankie ran into the Fab and slammed the door behind her. The sudden breeze blew Justin Bieber's face right off the skeleton—just another normie who couldn't stand to look at her.

"Frankie, the asparagus, *please*," Viveka called from the head of the table, this time a little louder, bringing Frankie back to the present.

"Oh, sorry." Frankie leaned forward to grab the white ceramic dish, and passed it across the table to Mrs. Mathis. But the plump woman with Hillary Clinton's hairstyle in Bill Clinton's hair color was too taken with Viktor's theory—on electromagnetic energy and how it could possibly give life to inanimate objects—to notice.

Mrs. Mathis tittered. "Did you hear that, Charles?" She slapped her sun-spotted chest. "Maybe you'll be able to marry that flat-screen TV after all."

"That's why we love this mad scientist." Dean Mathis reached behind his wife and squeezed Viktor's shoulder. "One day he's going to invent something that will change the way we live forever."

If only he had the electromagnetic courage to tell Dean Mathis that the "something" had already been invented and was passing his wife a plate of asparagus.

"He already did," Frankie announced, lowering the dish.

"Is that so?" The dean sat back on the brushed-aluminum chair and stroked the sides of his salt-and-pepper beard. "And what might that be?"

"Me." Frankie beamed with all the charm of a modern-day Shirley Temple.

The dean and his wife burst out laughing. Viktor and Viveka did not.

"Asparagus, anyone?"

"None for me, Viv, thanks." Mrs. Mathis waved it away.

"Cora can't stand vegetables," the dean explained.

"Now, Charles." She turned to look at him directly. "You know that's not true. Just the green ones. There's something about that color....It's not very appetizing. Am I right?"

Frankie sparked.

Viktor cleared his throat.

"Anyone for seconds?" Viveka asked.

"What's *that*?" Mrs. Mathis asked.

Frankie found it hard to believe that plump Mrs. Mathis wasn't familiar with *seconds*. Then she noticed that the woman's ruby-ringed finger was pointing at the front door, where a red chenille glove was poking a piece of paper through the mail slot.

"What in the world...?" Viktor got up and threw open the door.

The two girls on the other side screamed.

Blue and Lala.

"Hey!" Frankie jumped up, eager to escape the dinner table. There was something about the color white that Frankie found so unappetizing.

"What's going on, girls?" Viktor asked, bending down to pick up the paper.

They exchanged a nervous look. "We, um, just wanted to drop off something for Frankie," Blue explained, her blond curls tied into low pigtails.

Frankie grabbed the paper from her father's hand. "A petition?"

"We're going to boycott the September Semi unless they

162

change the Monster Mash theme," Lala explained, shivering inside her bubblegum-pink cashmere cowl-necked sweater. "But don't worry," she whispered to Viktor. "We're saying we don't like the theme because it's too scary, not because it's offensive." She obviously didn't care about breaking the no-talking-about-RAD-business-even-in-RADs-only-conversations rule.

"I don't want to boycott," Frankie insisted, thinking of Brett and the dinner cruise they could win. "I want to go. I wanna put the *boy* in *boycott*," she said, dancing.

"What about the theme?" Blue asked, ignoring Frankie's boycott dance. "Doesn't it make you mad as a cut snake?"

A gust of wind blew leaves and other suburban tumbleweed around the cul-de-sac.

"Wanna come in?" Frankie offered.

"Um, that's not the best idea." Viktor gripped the door handle. "We have company."

"We can go in my room," Frankie suggested.

"Another time." Viktor squinted a grave warning in response. "Good night, girls."

He shut the door in their faces without giving them the chance to say good-bye.

"What are you *doing*?" Frankie pulled the suffocating turtleneck-scarf combo away from her neck.

"Viktor," Viveka's raised voice called from the dining room. "What's the name of that crazy roommate you had in college? The one who removed his own appendix?"

"Tommy Lassman," Viktor called back, still squinting.

"Oh, that's right!" Viveka laughed and then continued telling her story.

"Why have you been testing us lately?" Viktor whispered.

"I'm not testing you." Frankie felt her edge soften for the first time all night. "I'm just frustrated."

"We understand how you feel, but acting out isn't the way to express it."

"Well, what is?" Frankie leaned against the cool concrete wall and folded her arms across her chest. "Signing a petition for the wrong cause? Acting like you're trying to invent things you already invented? Trying to get research money for a normie cause when your own people are—"

"That's *enough*!" Viktor clapped his hands together.

Frankie jumped at the thunderous sound.

"Is that another storm I hear?" Mrs. Mathis asked. "This rain has been relentless."

Normally, Frankie and her father would have cracked up at the woman's misconception. But they both knew this situation was far from funny.

"You may as well sign that petition, because you're not going to the dance."

"*What?*" Frankie stomped her Pour La Victoire knee-high boot on the spotless white floor. "What does the dance have to do with—"

"You need to learn discretion. And until you do, I can't trust you."

"I'll be discreet, I promise," Frankie said sincerely. "Trust me."

"I'm sorry, Frankie, but it's too late."

Is he really doing this?

"What was the point of giving me life if you're not going to let me live it?" she cried.

"That's enough," he mumbled.

"No, I'm serious," Frankie insisted, fed up with being silenced. "Why didn't you just make me a normie?"

Viktor sighed. "Because that's not who we are. We're special. And I'm very proud of that. You should be too."

"Proud?" Frankie spat out the word as if it had been soaked in nail polish remover. "How can I be proud when everyone is telling me to hide?"

"I'm telling you to hide so you'll be safe. But you can still feel proud of who you are," he explained, like it was really that simple. "Pride has to come from within you and stay with you, no matter what people say."

Huh?

Frankie crossed her arms and looked away.

"I built your brain and body. Strength and confidence have to come from you," Viktor explained, as if sensing her confusion.

"How do I get it?" Frankie asked.

"You had it the morning we took you to Mount Hood High," he reminded her. "Before you let those cheerleaders take it away."

"How do I get it back?" Frankie wondered aloud.

"It might take a while," he said, his squinty eyes peering over her shoulder to check on his guests. "But when you find it, hold on to it with all your might. And don't let anyone take it away, no matter how hard they try. Understand?"

Frankie nodded, even though she didn't.

"Good." Viktor winked.

The confusing lesson whipped Frankie's anger into something she had never felt before. It was like an emotional meringue—the airy feeling of loneliness topped with the hard crisp of injustice. Yet its taste was far from sweet.

Viktor strolled back into the dining room, arms swinging casually at his sides. "Who's ready for dessert?"

Frankie hurried for her bedroom, not caring who saw or what they thought of her. Not caring about caring at all. The instant her hand gripped the door handle, she began sobbing. She slid her back down the wall, sat on the cold floor, and buried her face in her hands. Thinking of the only person she knew who saw the beauty in monsters.

The September Semi was her big opportunity to mingle with Brett—and to help him get to know the real Frankie.

Which he would, shortly after she gave him a makeup remover pad…

"Go ahead," she would say, once they convened under the stairwell. Thumping music would bleed from the gym into the empty hallway and attempt to entice them back onto the dance floor. But they would resist, opting for the a cappella rhythm of their beating hearts instead. "Wipe my cheek," she would say.

He would rub his black-polished fingers across the coarse pad and deem it too abrasive for her tender flesh. But she would insist. And so he would comply.

His loving touch would bring a tear to her eye.

The discovery of her mint-green skin would bring a tear to his.

"Why didn't you tell me?" he would ask.

She would lower her eyes in shame. "Are you mad?"

"Yes."

Another tear.

After wiping it away, he would lift her chin with his finger and say, "I'm mad about you."

A passionate life-changing kiss would follow. Then they would enter the gym for one more dance, and exit with the prize for best couple's costume. Their love would blossom on the dinner cruise. And soon he would be wearing her face on his T-shirts. Her natural mint beauty would appeal to millions—even Mrs. Mathis. By Christmas there would be a clothing line called Frankie.... Toy companies would make Frankie dolls.... M&M's would only come in green....

Frankie stopped, no longer satisfied with daydreams and promises of a better tomorrow. Maybe her father was right not to trust her. Maybe she wasn't Daddy's perfect little girl anymore. Because Daddy's perfect little girl would do what she was told. She would skip the September Semi and practice discretion.

But Frankie didn't see the point in doing that.

CHAPTER EIGHTEEN
TOO HOT TO HANDLE

Haylee followed Bekka down the "Till Death Do You Part" aisle of the Costume Castle like a dutiful maid of honor. Melody followed Haylee like a jealous bridesmaid.

"What about this one?" Haylee lifted a sleek wedding dress off the rack.

"Too shiny," Bekka said.

Haylee held up another one.

"Too lacy."

"This?"

"Too poufy."

"This?"

"Too white."

"Maybe you should go as Bridezilla instead," Melody grumbled.

"Maybe you should go as the Sulk Ness Monster," Bekka countered.

Melody couldn't help giggling at her friend's goofy retort.

Bekka giggled too. Then she got right back to business. "I want scary-sexy-cool."

"This?" Haylee tried.

"Too frumpy."

"This?"

"Too costumey."

"Bekka, we *are* at a costume store," Melody pointed out.

"Good point." Bekka reached for her necklace and slid the gold *B* charm back and forth on its chain. "So maybe you should be thinking about your own outfit. The Monster Mash is next Friday. And since today is Saturday, that gives you less than a week to—"

"Stop." Melody rolled her tired eyes. "I already told you. I'm not going."

"Why? Because you and Jackson got into some silly fight last night?"

Haylee held up the last wedding dress.

"Too sweet."

"It wasn't *silly*," Melody snapped, wishing she had never mentioned it. How could she possibly explain something she barely understood herself? Jackson's behavior left her with a feeling, not a story. And *gutted* was the only way to describe it.

"Fine, then go with someone else," Haylee said, pinching the tulle on a cobweb veil and rubbing it between her fingers.

"Ew, I swear I just saw flames. I wonder if they have better quality in the back," Bekka said. "Hmmmm." She looked up at the massive spiders hanging from the ceiling and tapped her chin. "Hayl, can you ask the—"

"I'm on it." Haylee hurried off in search of a manager. Her tiny butt moved with windup-toy efficiency.

"So, do you have *any* costume ideas?" Bekka asked, trying to sound helpful and supportive.

"How about the Invisible Girl?" Melody ran her hand along the packs of waxy Halloween makeup. Colors called bat black, bloodred, ghoulish green, and phantom white stood at the ready inside their plastic casings. Melody leaned close and sniffed. They didn't smell anything like Jackson's pastels. They were sweeter, less intense. But tears gathered anyway.

"Knock knock," Bekka said, checking the price of a black garter.

"Who's there?" Melody sniffed.

"Boo."

"Boo who?"

"Since you've been making that sound all morning, why don't you go as a depressed ghost?"

Melody giggle-sniffed. "It's not funny."

"Then why are you laugh-*ing*?" Bekka said in a singsong.

"I'm no-*ot*," Melody sang back.

"Fine." Bekka stepped away from the thirty-four-dollar wedding dresses and folded her arms across her denim utility jacket. "If you don't go, I don't go."

"Yeah, right." Melody flicked Bekka's arm playfully. "And miss the chance to be Brett's bride?"

"Friends first," she insisted, her green eyes fixed and sure.

"I can't let you do that."

"Then it looks like you're going." Bekka's freckled face radiated victory.

Haylee returned, her hurried stride full of purpose. "I spoke to Gavin, the assistant manager. He said they aren't expecting any more Bride of Frankenstein dresses until mid-October. But he gave me"—she peeked at the business card in her hand—"Dan Mooney's number. He's the manager and will be back on Monday. So we can double-check with him."

Haylee's dedication to Bekka tickled Melody's insides. They weren't typical tenth graders, but they were loyal. And Melody had grown to adore them for both those reasons.

"Nah, it's okay." Bekka sighed, surrendering to the selection. "I'll make up for it with awesome hair."

"Then I recommend the shiny one," Haylee said, pulling it off the rack. "It's simple and elegant, and my Flower Ghoul dress is shiny too, so it will look well thought out."

"Brilliant!" Bekka laid the dress over her arm. "Now all we need is…" Her eyes wandered. "Heyyyyy, look who it is…."

"Hey." Melody heard a familiar boy's voice.

She turned. It was Deuce. Despite the low lighting, he wore a pair of dark red Ray-Bans and an Ed Hardy trucker hat. Seeing him made her lips thirst for gloss. It was their way of telling her they'd rather sit this one out. Melody shut her mouth, assuring them she would too.

"Hey." He smiled awkwardly. Hefty Bose headphones were clamped to his ears, and he made no attempt to remove them.

"What brings you here?" Bekka asked like a nosy mom.

Haylee began typing.

"Uh, costume shopping." He raised his metal shopping basket. Assuming she had failed to notice his hat selection, he said, "I'm going to be the Mad Hatter."

"And Cleo?" Bekka pressed.

Melody resisted the urge to smack her.

Deuce shifted uncomfortably. "She's not going this year."

"Trouble in paradise?"

"*Bekka!*" Melody snapped. "It's none of our business."

"Actually, we're cool." Deuce smiled weakly. "It's just that some of her friends were thinking of passing this year, so she's probably going to hang with them and—"

"So you're going solo?"

"Maybe. I'm not completely—"

"Perfect!" Bekka clapped her hands. "Why don't you and Melly go together?"

"Bekka!" Melody stomped her black Converse. Inside, the ticklish feeling quickly turned to scratching.

"What?" Bekka asked innocently, feigning interest in a blood-soaked bouquet. "It'll be fun. Don'tcha think, Deuce?"

"Yeah, it would." He nodded, warming to the idea. "But just as friends, cuz, you know, Cleo and—"

"Of course!" Bekka negotiated.

"Okay." Deuce smiled sweetly.

"Get out your iPhone," Bekka insisted. "I'll bump you Melody's number."

"I'm right here, you know," Melody seethed.

"One-two-threeeeee...BUMP!" Bekka and Deuce knocked phones.

"Got it," Deuce said to his screen. Then, to Melody, "I'll text you day of."

"Cool." Melody grinned, her mouth still closed.

The short bike ride back from the Costume Castle was mostly

173

silent. Optimistically sunny, the blue sky seemed to challenge Melody the same way Bekka had, making it almost impossible for her to wallow. Every few blocks, Bekka would assure Melody that she was only trying to help. And Melody would say she appreciated it but she hadn't asked for help. And then more silence.

"This is me," Melody announced as they approached the top of Radcliffe Way.

"You still don't have a costume," Bekka called.

"I still don't care." Melody waved good-bye, partially smiling despite herself.

Hurrying past her mother and the bottles of wine she was setting out on the table, Melody stomped up the wooden steps to her room.

"We're having some neighbors over for a wine-tasting class in an hour," Glory called up the stairs. "In case you were wondering."

Melody slammed her bedroom door, letting her mother know she wasn't.

"I have your fan," Candace called from her bedroom. "I'll bring it back when my toenails are dry."

"Whatever," Melody mumbled.

She climbed the ladder to her loft bed and flopped, belly first, onto her lavender and lilac Roxy duvet. After the first wave of sobs passed, she rolled over and stared at the wood rafters on her ceiling.

Her iPhone chirped. She had a text. It was from Deuce.

DEUCE: I forgot to ask about your costume.

Melody tossed her phone aside without responding. Was she really going to the dance with *Deuce*? The thought of a pity date with someone else's boyfriend felt lonelier than going alone.

Even with open windows, the heat in the house was unbearable, something Beau had been trying to have fixed for weeks. Not that Melody really cared. She was numb all over. If it hadn't been for the sweat on her forehead, she wouldn't have even noticed.

She began to wallow all over again. Sweat brought back memories of the previous night...being under the ThermaFoil...kissing Jackson...

"Hey," she heard him say.

She shot up and bumped her forehead on a beam.

"You okay?" He put his hand on a black rung of the ladder.

Melody nodded, unable to speak.

There he was. Glasses. Shy smile. Green short-sleeved buttondown. Pastel-stained fingertips. As if nothing had ever happened. "It's so hot in here." He fanned his face.

"Then leave." She flopped back down on her back.

"I don't want to," he protested.

"Well, what *do* you want, then?"

"I came by to tell you that last night was fun," he said.

"Yeah, until it wasn't."

He sighed. "I blacked out again, didn't I?"

"More like perved out, Jackson." Melody sat up. She hung her legs off the edge of her bed, leaned back on her hands, and faced her closet. Looking at him was almost as impossible as forgiving him. "And stop with this whole blacking-out excuse, okay? It's insulting. Go try it on *Firecracker*. Maybe she's bimbo enough to believe it, 'cause I'm not!"

175

"It's true," he pleaded. "I came to by the house in the cul-de-sac."

"Well, you should have stayed there."

"If I did, you wouldn't have a date for the September Semi," he said, trying to be cute.

"Yes, I would," she said, trying to hurt him. "I'm going with Deuce."

He didn't respond. Mission accomplished.

"Melody." Jackson went to the foot of the bed and grabbed her swinging feet. "The last thing I remember is kissing you under that blanket. After that I—"

"Trust me, Jackson." She finally looked at him. His face was covered in sweat, shame, and confusion. "You're not blacking out. I almost wish you had."

"Then why don't I remember anything?" He wiped his forehead.

"You do. You just use this blackout thing as an excuse to say what you want and kiss who you want and—"

Jackson removed his glasses and unbuttoned his shirt, giving Melody a backstage pass to his glistening boy-band abs.

"What are you doing?" She reached for her iPhone. Involving the police was not out of the question, and she began recording just in case she needed proof.

"You again?" He lifted his brows. "I should have known from all this sweat." He ran his fingers along his chest. "Girl, you make me *hottttttt*."

"Jackson, enough!" Melody jumped down from her bed.

"Why do you keep calling me Jackson?"

"Because that's your name," Melody insisted, holding her white iPhone to his face.

"No, it isn't."

"Really?" Melody challenged. "What is it, then?"

"D.J.," he said right to the lens. "D.J. Hyde. As in Dr. Jekyll and Mr. Hyde. Just like my great-grandfather...who was super-freaky, by the way. I found some papers in our attic, and it looks like he did all these weird experiments with tonics back in the day—experiments on *himself*! After he drank these potions, he turned into quite a wild man. I'm not into drinking, but I do like a good dance party." He winked and then looked around the messy room. "Got any music?"

Melody ended her recording. Before she could stop him, D.J. Hyde had hurried toward the white docking station on her desk and attached his own iPhone. "Carry Out" by Timbaland came blasting from her speakers. Swiveling his hips and spreading his arms so his shirt looked like wings, he began dancing as if performing for a stadium full of screaming girls.

"What's going on in here?" Candace appeared in the doorway holding Melody's fan. Barefoot, dressed in baggy boyfriend jeans and a tight white tank, she had the whole lazy-sexy look down. "Are you shooting an audition tape for something?"

"Yeah, it's a little show I like to call And Who Might You Be?" He removed the fan from her arms and pulled her toward him.

"Candace." She giggled, allowing herself to be taken.

Timbaland's beats came at them like balls in a batting cage, and D.J. returned each one with an overhead snap of his fingers.

"Melly, who knew?" Candace called above the music. Then she raised her hands above her head too.

"Not me." Melody plugged in the fan.

"Wind machine!" D.J. shouted.

Suddenly, he and Candace were gyrating in front of the fan. D.J.'s blowing shirt made them look as if they were actually inside Timbaland's video.

"Whoooo-hooooooo!" Candace shouted, her hands now turning tight circles above her head. She leaned over and cranked up the speed of the fan.

D.J. held out his hands like Superman. "I'm flying!" he announced as his shirt billowed behind him like a cape.

"What's going on up there?" Glory called.

"Nothing," Melody answered. The truth was impossible to explain.

"Well, turn that *nothing* down, please. My guests will be here any minute."

More than happy to put an end to the party, Melody quickly removed the iPhone from the dock.

It took a few seconds for Candace and D.J. to stop dancing. A few more for them to stop laughing. And a few more for the room to cool down.

"That was awesome." Candace high-fived her dance partner. "You're much more fun than you look."

"'Scuse me?" He put on his glasses, sounding slightly confused.

"Those glasses and that shirt." Candace pointed at his chest. "You know, when it's buttoned." She giggled. "They make you seem kind of nerdy. But you're fun."

He looked down and quickly fastened his buttons. "I am?"

Melody felt the sting of clarity zip up her spine. "What's your name?"

"Huh?"

"What's your name?" she pressed.

"Jackson." He backed up, leaned against her ladder, and rubbed his slick forehead. "Oh no. Did I just have another blackout?"

"Oh yeah," Melody said. "Only you didn't black out." She stood beside him and pressed PLAY on her iPhone. "Jackson, meet D.J. Hyde."

"Jackson, wait!" Melody called. But he didn't listen.

After seeing the way he had acted in front of Melody, he hurried off faster than the paparazzi on a Britney lead.

Candace didn't say a word. All she did was glare at Melody and shake her head disapprovingly.

"*What?*"

"Exactly." Candace lifted her blond hair and fanned the back of her neck.

"Exactly *what*?" Melody snapped, her thoughts smudged and whirling like Jackson's carousel sketch.

"What are you going to do about it?"

"What *can* I do?" Melody glanced at the unpacked boxes in her room. Maybe she could tackle those. "I don't think it's a call-the-police kind of thing."

"Maybe you should go after him," Candace suggested, like someone who actually cared.

"No, thanks." Melody picked a loose cuticle until it bled. "A relationship with an unpredictable...whateverthatwas...is not the kind of thing I'm looking for right now."

"Well then, you're missing out." Candace turned to leave, her butt splashing around inside the excess denim of her saggy jeans.

"Wait!"

Candace froze.

"What do you mean, I'm missing out?" Melody asked.

"Unpredictable is fun!" Candace said, like she knew firsthand. "Even if Jackson's only around half the time, you're still ahead of most girls."

Melody thought of him and smiled. "He's nice, isn't he?"

"Go find him," Candace insisted, her aqua-blue eyes radiating sincerity. "Because that's what sticking with something means." She snapped her fingers. "Love Doctor out."

Melody raced down the stairs and pushed past the tall couple in her doorway.

"Sweetheart, I'd like you to meet the Steins from down the street. They have a daughter your age—"

"Nice to meet you," Melody called over her shoulder. "I'll be home soon."

"Don't worry," the woman with the long black hair told Glory. "My daughter is the same way."

Charging toward the white cottage, Melody felt like a romantic-comedy cliché—racing to the airport before her jilted lover's plane took off. But that's where the similarities ended. As far as she knew, the girl chasing after a jilted crazy had not been done.

The door to his house was open a crack. "Jackson?" she gently called. "Jackson?" She pushed the door with her index finger. An icy blast of air stung her hand. Melody stepped inside. It couldn't have been more than sixty degrees. Were thermostats in Salem really so difficult to control?

At first Melody thought better of barging into Jackson's home, especially since his mother was her science teacher, but he had done it to her twice, so...

"Jackson?" she called softly.

Dusty velvet couches, dark Oriental rugs, and cluttered corners filled with knickknacks that could have arrived via time machine from Old World London cramped the small space. And bogged it down with a sense of historical weariness—an unexpected contrast to the bright, cheery innocence of the exterior. Melody smiled to herself. It was a contrast she knew all too well.

"If you knew who I was, why didn't you tell me?" Jackson shouted from somewhere on the second floor.

Melody heard his mother's voice. "I wanted to protect you!" she insisted.

Melody knew she should leave but couldn't.

"From *what*?" Jackson sobbed. "Waking up in strange yards? Making a fool of myself at the neighbors' house? Freaking out the only girl I've ever really liked?"

Melody couldn't help smiling. He *really* liked her.

"Because you haven't protected me from any of that!" Jackson continued. "It's all happened. And that was just in the past twenty-four hours! Who knows what I've done in the last fifteen years."

"That's the whole point," his mother explained. "This hasn't been going on for fifteen years. It started to get worse as you got older."

They were silent for a second.

"What triggers it?" Jackson asked, sounding calmer.

"Overheating," Ms. J said softly.

Melody shuffled through the memories of her D.J. encounters. *Of course!* ThermaFoil...her bedroom...the fan...

"Overheating," Jackson repeated calmly. As though he should have known it all along. "That's why it's always so cold in here."

"And why I never let you play sports," Ms. J explained, sounding relieved to·share her secret.

"But why heat?"

"Jackson, sit down for a second." There was a pause. "I've never told you this, but your great-grandfather was Dr. Jekyll.... He was a shy, gentle man, just like you. But sometimes his shyness held him back. So he created a potion that gave him courage, and made him more...forceful. He became dependent on it, and eventually...it killed him."

"But how did I—" Jackson began.

His mother cut him off. "The potion was toxic and ended up corrupting his DNA. And the trait was passed down. Your grandfather and father had it too."

"So Dad didn't abandon us?"

"No." Her voice cracked. "We met when I was a genetic research scientist, and...I did everything I could." She sniffed. "But the mood swings became intolerable, and it...well, it drove him mad!"

Jackson didn't respond. Ms. J was silent. The only sounds coming from the upstairs room were sniffles and heartbreaking whimpers.

Melody cried too. For Jackson. For his mother. For his ancestors. And for herself.

"Is that going to happen to me?" he finally asked.

"No." Ms. J blew her nose. "It's different with you. Perhaps it's mutating. But it seems to affect you only when you get too hot. Once you cool down, you shift back."

There was a long pause.

"So are you like, his"—he paused—"...his mother too?"

"I am," she answered matter-of-factly. "Because he is you... only different."

"Different how?"

"D.J. is comfortable in the spotlight, whereas you tend to be more shy. He loves music; you love art. He is confident, while you're thoughtful. You are both terrific in your own way."

"Does he know about me?"

"No." She paused. "But he knows who his ancestors are."

"How—"

Ms. J cut him off. "D.J. has done some digging into his past, but he doesn't know about you. He thinks he has blackouts too. He can't be trusted. No one can. You have to keep this to yourself. Promise me. Can you do that?"

Melody took that as her cue to slip out. She didn't want to hear Jackson's answer. She had heard too much already.

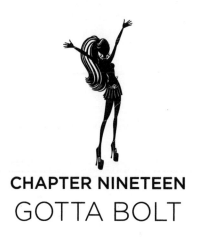

CHAPTER NINETEEN
GOTTA BOLT

Plan A was ready for activation. After a week of intense prepping and planning, it was the most respectable way for Frankie to get to the September Semi. But it wasn't the only way.

"Mom, Dad, can I talk to you for a minute?" she asked, fresh from her evening charge and aromatherapy *seam*-steam.

They were on the sofa, listening to jazz and reading by the fire. Their Fierce & Flawless had been removed, and their neck bolts were exposed. Dinner had been made (thanks to Frankie), the dishes had been cleaned (thanks to Frankie), and there had been no indiscretions for seven whole days (thanks to Frankie).

It was time.

"What's up?" Viktor put down his medical journal and took his worn UGGs off the ottoman: an invitation to sit.

"Um..." Frankie felt her neck seams. They were loose and relaxed from their steam.

"Don't tug," Viveka warned. Her violet eyes ripened to an

eggplant purple against her green skin. It seemed criminal that others couldn't enjoy how naturally beautiful she was.

"Are you nervous about something?" Viktor asked.

"Nope." Frankie sat on her hands. "I just wanted to say that I thought a lot about my behavior last week and I agree with you. It was dangerous and insensitive."

The corners of their mouths turned up just a smidge, as if they were unwilling to commit to a full smile until they knew where this conversation was going.

"Just like you asked, I came right home from school every day, I didn't text, e-mail, tweet, or post on Facebook. And during lunch, I only spoke when spoken to."

All of which was true. She'd even avoided eye contact with Brett. Which hadn't been too hard, since Bekka had switched seats with him in science class.

"We know." Viktor leaned forward and double-tapped her knee. "And we couldn't be more proud."

Viveka nodded in agreement.

"Thank you." Frankie humbly lowered her eyes. *One...two... three...GO!*

"Sodoyouthinkyoucouldtrustmetogotothedancetonight?" she blurted before losing her nerve.

Viktor and Viveka exchanged a quick glance.

Are they considering it? They are! They trust—

"No," they said together.

Frankie resisted the urge to spark. Or scream. Or threaten to go on a charging strike. She had prepared herself for this. It had always been a possibility. That's why she'd read *Acting for Young*

Actors: The Ultimate Teen Guide by Mary Lou Belli and Dinah Lenney. So that she could *act* like she understood their rejection. *Act* like she accepted it. And *act* like she would return to her room with grace. "Well, thanks for hearing me out," she said, kissing them on the cheeks and skipping off to bed. "Good night."

"Good *night*?" Viktor responded. "That's it? No argument?"

"No argument," Frankie said with a sweet smile. "You have to see this punishment through or you're not teaching me anything. I get it."

"O-*kay*." Viktor returned to his medical journal, shaking his head as if he couldn't quite believe what he was hearing.

"We love you." Viveka blew another kiss.

"I love you too." Frankie blew two back.

Time for Plan B.

"All right, Glitterati," Frankie said, taking her glitter-dusted confidants into the lounge area of the Fab. "This isn't going to be pretty. Rules will be broken. Friendships will be tested. And huge risks will be taken. But they're small prices to pay for true love and personal freedom, right?" She placed their cage on her orange-lacquered side table. They clawed the glass in agreement.

Blasting Lady Gaga's "Just Dance," Frankie tore open a box of hair bleach and painted chunky white streaks from her scalp to her ends. Spaced four inches apart, they would look just like her grandmother's. While waiting for them to set, she reclined on her red pillow-covered Moroccan chaise and began texting Lala. "Here goes." She sighed.

187

FRANKIE: Still boycotting?

LALA: Yup. Cleo, Clawdeen, and Blue r here. Love that ur txting again. ☺ Sure u can't come over?

FRANKIE: punished ☹

"This is the semi-manipulative part," Frankie told the Glitter-ati. "I've saved this secret all week, and it needs to be released." She typed a message and then hit SEND. "Don't judge me."

FRANKIE: FYI my parents were at that new girl Melody's last weekend for some wine-tasting party and heard she was going to Semi w/ Deuce.

LALA: FYI they rented that house from my grandparents, u know.

That was hardly the response she'd been hoping for.

FRANKIE: Cool about ur grandparents' place. Think it's true about Deuce? Does Cleo know?

Silence... silence... silence... silence... silence... It was 6:50 PM. The dance would be starting in forty minutes. Where was—

CLEO: Is this true?

She sat up. *Yes!*

FRANKIE: That's what my mom said.
FRANKIE: Wanna bust them?
CLEO: Totally but we don't have costumes. ☹

Yes! Yes! Yes! "It's working!" Frankie told the Glitterati. She felt a certain degree of guilt for manipulating the situation. But everything she was saying was true. And her reasons for saying them were for her friends' benefit as much as hers. Eventually, they would thank her. Everyone would. She just had to get them there.

FRANKIE: It's Monster Mash! We were born in costumes! Amazing, glorious costumes.

FRANKIE: This is our big chance to see what people think of us. The real us.

FRANKIE: We have to show em there's nothing to be afraid of.

FRANKIE: If we don't get over our fears they never will.

It was time to take a break before her friends accused her of sounding like a bumper sticker. But it was hard not to preach. She had never felt so strongly about anything. Not even Brett.

Silence...silence...silence...silence...silence...silence... silence...silence...silence...silence...silence...silence... silence...silence...silence...silence...silence...silence... silence...silence...silence...silence...silence...silence... silence...

"What are they doing?" Frankie lay back down and sparked.

Silence...silence...silence...silence...silence...silence... silence...silence...silence...silence...silence...silence...

silence ... silence ... silence ... silence ... silence ... silence ...
silence ... silence ... silence ... silence ... silence ... silence ...
silence ...

CLEO: Aren't u grounded?
FRANKIE: I'll sneak out bedroom window.

Silence ... silence ... silence ... silence ... silence ... silence ...
silence ... silence ... silence ... silence ... silence ...

LALA: Meet u at the top of Radcliffe in 5.
LALA: This better work.
FRANKIE: ☺

She bicycled her moccasin-covered feet in the air. *Yes! Yes! Yes!*

Frankie blew a kiss to the Glitterati, turned off the music, and grabbed the garment bag she had pulled from the garage. Wearing nothing but sweats and a sheer coat of lip gloss, she wiggled through her frosted window and jumped the six feet to freedom, feeling more charged than a Visa card at Christmastime.

CHAPTER TWENTY
IS THIS FREAK TAKEN?

"Okay, one more picture!" Bekka's father hurried out of the red Cadillac SRX. He was dressed in a burgundy fleece, Dockers, and blue slippers.

"Dad!" Bekka stomped her satin stilettos. She pointed at the school's front steps, which were spotted with giant green footprints and flecked with costumed kids acting too cool to enter the dance. Fog seeped from the blacked-out double doors, dragging thumping bass beats with it. "Brett's waiting for me inside."

"It's okay." Melody put her arms around Bekka and Haylee. "One more picture won't kill us."

"No," Bekka mumbled as a cluster of senior cheerleader zombies skipped by. "But the embarrassment will."

"Smile!" Mr. Madden insisted, lifting his glasses onto his bald head.

Bekka and Haylee complied. Melody tried. Recovering from facial surgery had been easier. Yes, she was healthy, almost asthma-free, and part of a loving family. But was it so much to ask for a relationship that lasted longer than a kiss?

All week Jackson had avoided her. Blaming homework or headaches, he had thwarted every one of Melody's requests for hang time. And like a respectful friend-slash-eavesdropper, she had said she understood. But Melody wanted to help. She wanted to be his shoulder to cry on. To share his burden. To tell him she had felt like a "monster" her whole life. To tell him that she understood. But obviously he didn't want her shoulder, or any of her other body parts. Which crushed her chest more than asthma ever had.

Alone in her box-filled room each night, Melody resisted the urge to confide in Candace. Jackson's secret was too damaging to share. Instead, she tried to convince herself that his distance had nothing to do with his Melody feelings and everything to do with the promise he'd made to his mother. But there was only so much self-love she could administer to the wound. After a while it just felt pathetic, like sending herself flowers on Valentine's Day.

Melody couldn't really shake off her mood, but she had managed to get herself dressed for the dance. She didn't want to let down her two new friends: the Bride of Frankenstein and her Flower Ghoul.

"You girls look great!" Mr. Madden gushed, shuffling back to his open car door. "I'll pick you up at ten, sharp," he announced, then drove away.

His taillights faded in the distance, taking away any hope Melody had of leaving early. Why had she agreed to leave her purse in the car? Bekka had said it would "free them up." *Ha!* It would do the opposite, by trapping her for two and a half hours with the wrong guy.

"Can you please try to have fun?" Bekka pleaded, as if reading her mind.

Melody promised she would. "You look great."

"I'd better." She sighed shakily, lifted her train, and began wobble-mounting the steps in her four-inch heels.

Bekka treated her role as Frankenstein's bride more like an audition to be Brett's bride. Every part of her body had been colored bright kelly green—even the parts that her mother had stressed were "not to be seen by anyone except God and the inside of a toilet bowl." Instead of wearing a wig, Bekka had teased and then shellacked her own hair into a windblown cone, and she'd used female-mustache bleach to create white streaks. Her seams, made of real suture thread, had been attached to her neck and wrists with clear double-sided costume tape because drawing them with kohl would not have been "honoring the character." Her Costume Castle dress had been exchanged for something more "authentic" from the Bridal Barn. If Brett didn't see his future in her heavily black-shadowed eyes tonight, he never would. Or so she believed.

"You look great too, Hayl," Melody added.

"Thanks." Haylee grinned, looking like a possessed child beauty pageant contestant. The Flower Ghoul wore a shiny yellow dress, white tights, and a face full of white, black, and red makeup. She carried a basket full of rubber insects.

No one complimented Melody on her costume. And if they did, she'd know they were lying. Dressed in black leggings, her mother's black Chanel blazer, black ballet flats, a beret, and a face full of red and black horror makeup, she was Freak Chic. Everyone agreed it was better than her Killer Wave idea.

The instant Bekka opened the school doors, Melody's chest constricted. "I can't go in there!"

A skeleton and a Cyclops entered instead.

"Melly, get over it, okay?" Bekka snapped.

"No," she said, wheezing. "The fog machine. My asthma. Puffer's in your dad's..."

"Just go!" Bekka pushed Melody through the thick layer of gray smoke and guided her toward the gym. She leaned on the silver pump-handle, and the door hissed open.

Darkness. Black lights. A Rihanna remix. Trash bags taped to the walls. Gigantic cocoons filled with fake dead people dangling from the ceiling pipes. The smell of rubber soles and duct tape. Snack tables divided into allergy zones and marked by gravestones. Round tables littered with fake body parts. Chairs wrapped in white sheets that were splattered in red paint. Costumed girls dancing on the dance floor. Costumed boys working up the courage to join them. As she struggled to breathe, these details rushed her senses, as if begging to be appreciated before she collapsed.

"Here." Bekka handed her an inhaler.

Melody took a big puff. "Ahhhhhhh..." She delighted in the steady exhale. "Where did you get that?"

"I took it from your purse before we left the car." She handed it to Melody. "Principal Weeks loves that machine. He even uses it on Thanksgiving. He says it was foggy the day the Pilgrims landed at Plymouth Rock."

"Thank you." Melody smiled and knit her brows at the same time. "If Brett doesn't propose to you tonight, I will."

"Forget the proposal. Just promise me you'll try to have a good time."

"I promise." Melody raised her palm. It was the least she could do.

Deuce approached them with a confident swagger.

"Here comes the Mad Hatter," Haylee announced.

Wearing a tall red velvet hat, a matching tuxedo, and his signature sunglasses, Deuce looked mad hot. Melody decided that if she had to be stuck at a dance with someone else's boyfriend while missing her wish-he'd-be-my-boyfriend, Deuce was the guy.

"Hey…crazy beret girl," he said, trying not to insult her ambiguous costume.

"I'm Freak Chic." She flicked her cap and then rolled her eyes at her own patheticness.

"Oh yeah, I kinda see that now." He smile-nodded.

"We're going to look for Brett and Heath," Bekka announced, then quickly took off with Haylee before Melody could stop them.

Suddenly left alone, they couldn't help but notice the fun all around them.

Monsters of every imaginable sort mingled, greeting one another with compliments and yanking reluctant partners toward the dance floor.

"So, what's with the shades?" Melody asked, trying to make conversation. "It's so dark in here. How do you see?" In the spirit of flirty party banter, she pulled them off.

"Give those back!" he shouted. He was so angry, he couldn't

even look at her. Instead, he looked past her shoulder, quickly shut his eyes, and then felt for his Oakleys as a blind man might.

"Here." Melody placed them in his tanned hands. He put them on with urgency. "Sorry, I was just—" She cut herself off. What *was* she doing, anyway?

"That's okay," Deuce said sweetly. "I should probably check in with Cleo. She's home alone and everything, so...you cool here for a minute?"

"Yeah, I'm fine."

"Great," Deuce said, accidentally knocking over a lone stone statue of a witch, and then sprinted for the exit.

After steadying the toppling witch (who looked a lot like a girl from her English class), Melody set out in search of Candace and, more important, cab fare. So what if she lived only three blocks away? Walking home alone from a dance was just as lame as couching it with Ben & Jerry's. If the feeling were an ice-cream flavor, it would be Sour Grapes.

Now that it was pushing eight o'clock, the too-cool-for-punctuality crowd ambled into the gym. With swaggers implying that they had other, more happening places to be, they examined the decorations like prospective buyers. Clinging to one another in clusters, they resisted the urge to bombard the dance floor when Jay-Z's "On to the Next One" began playing, making it next to impossible for Melody to spot Candace, who was dressed as a Scary Fairy. Most brunettes used costume parties as an opportunity to go blond, and blonds never went brunette, so this was a needle-in-a-haystack situation, at best.

While searching the Vegan Zone for her sister, Melody found

an elaborate meat-free spread that included baby carrots labeled GOBLIN FINGERS and tofu chunks called BEAST TEETH.

"Blood punch?" offered someone behind her.

His voice was soft but far from weak. Similar to a tone she recognized, but infused with an added kick of confidence. It was as though improvements had been made to the original model, and she was about to meet version 2.0.

D.J.?

Melody quickly turned. Red liquid splattered all over her face.

"Oh, gosh, I'm so sorry!" D.J. (or was it Jackson?) grabbed the stack of black cocktail napkins beside the bowl of Fritos marked DEMON FINGERNAILS.

"It's okay." Melody wiped her face. "I needed a good excuse to take this makeup off my face."

He instantly became a human tissue box, presenting a steady stream of napkins with the utmost reliability. Once the liquid had been absorbed and the napkins tossed into the bin marked MASH TRASH, they exchanged a warm smile that felt like returning home after a long trip.

"Jackson?"

He nodded sweetly.

"What are you doing here?" Melody asked, relieved. "Not that you don't have a right to be here or anything. I just...you know...you've been so busy lately."

"I thought you might wanna hump." He pointed to the pillow stuffed up under the back of his sweater like a hunchback.

"Oh." Melody's elevated spirits nose-dived. Grabbing his

wrist, she led him to an empty table and whispered, "D.J.? Is that you?"

"*No.*" Jackson reddened. "It was a joke. I thought you could use some cheering up, that's all."

"Me? Why *me?*"

"I kind of saw Deuce take off, and I know he was your date and everything."

Melody gasped, trying to seem offended. But he was struggling to look concerned about her date leaving, and failing as a smile kept tugging on his lips. He seemed adorably pleased with his discovery that she was now available. And, truth be told, Melody was too. "You were spying on me?"

He lifted a green plastic doll arm off the table and shook it in front of her face. "I learned it from you!"

"*Me?*"

"So, you *weren't* spying on me that night I found you in Candace's room?"

Melody opened her mouth to defend herself but burst out laughing instead. He laughed with her and then grabbed her hand. A warm current passed from his body into hers, and from hers to his, like electrical sockets that were joined.

"So, did you come here to tear me and Deuce apart?" Melody teased.

He ran a hand through his long layers and looked out at the whirling monsters on the dance floor. "I wanted to make sure he was treating you properly, that's all."

She squeezed her appreciation into his hand. He squeezed back "anytime."

Surrounded by the giddy din of party noise, Melody felt like a water balloon at a helium party. Bogged down by the burden of knowing his secret. And bothered by his unwillingness to share it. With each day that passed, it would become harder and harder to connect with him. Their secrets would eventually come between them, forcing them apart like magnets of the same pole.

He ran his finger over the fake blood on the chair.

She smiled awkwardly.

He smiled back.

Now what? There was so much to say, but no good way to bring it up. No natural segue. No transition sentence. No way to justify a cutesy opener like, "Speaking of eavesdropping..."

"Speaking of eavesdropping..." she tried anyway.

"Huh?" He snickered in his usual way—a mix of fascination and bewilderment. The way one might watch millipedes mate.

"So, you know how you caught me spying? And now I caught you spying?"

"Well, you didn't exactly *catch* me spying. I came forward and—"

"Okay, even better." Melody closed her eyes and took a deep breath. "Because I am coming forward to tell you that..." She took a quick puff of her inhaler. "You know how you walked into my house a few times without calling?"

He nodded.

"Well, I kind of did that to you."

She waited, hoping he'd react. Or maybe even figure out what she was trying to say, and finish the story for her. But he stared at her expectantly. Offering no easy way out.

"I know everything. IheardyouandyourmomtalkingandIcould haveleftbutIdidn'tbecauseIwantedtoknow." She sucked in a breath. "I wanted to understand."

Melody's heart thumped with the bass from the speakers. *Say something!*

Jackson looked at the gym floor and stood slowly. He was leaving.

"I have one thing to say." He reached inside the front pocket of his jeans.

Melody's chest began to tighten. She took another hit from her inhaler. It didn't help.

"*What?* Just tell me."

He pulled out a battery-operated mini-fan and flicked the switch. The white plastic blade began spinning around the blue base. It sounded like a bee. "This thing is the best!"

"*Huh?*" Melody half-laughed. "Did you even hear what I said?"

Nodding, he leaned back and closed his eyes, luxuriating in the paltry breeze.

"Jackson, I know your secret," she insisted. "I eavesdropped."

"What do you want me to do?" He leaned forward. "Send you to your room?"

"No, but—"

"It's okay." He grinned. "I already know."

"You do?"

"I left the door open for a reason," he said coolly. "And I saw you running back to your house."

"You did! Why didn't you tell me?"

"I wanted to make sure you were okay with it. I didn't want

you to feel like you owed me anything. It's kind of a heavy secret to carry around, you know?"

"Is that how you got that hump on your back?"

He laughed.

She laughed.

And then they waited for a slow song and danced.

Cheek to cheek, they swayed to Taylor Swift, a true Monster Mash in a gym of imposters. The invisible repellent force was gone. The only thing between them now was the soft breeze of Jackson's mini-fan.

CHAPTER TWENTY-ONE
HEAD OVER HEELS

Standing outside the double gym doors, Frankie, Lala, Blue, Clawdeen, and Cleo locked hands like the Pussycat Dolls about to take their final curtain call. They'd worked up their nerve on the drive over. Perfected one another's outfits in the parking lot. And declared this outing a small step for monster-kind. Now all they had to do was work up the courage to go inside before the dance was over.

"Okay, when I count to three." Frankie rolled back her shoulders, which were semi-visible thanks to Grandma Frankenstein's delicate lace wedding gown. "One...two..."

Suddenly the doors flew open. And like a vicious Red Rover opponent, someone tore through the girls' arms and broke their bond.

"Deuce?" Cleo gasped, her gold chandelier earrings swinging underneath her straight black hair. Her body was wrapped head to toe in white linen and adorned in a lavish blend of turquoise and gold jewelry. Made of solid gold, her snake-shaped crown

with the ruby eyes could double as a weapon, and she wasn't afraid to use it on two-timing guys. Or so she had said in the car.

"Hey," he stammered, adjusting his velvet top hat. "I was just running out to call you. I thought you were at home...boycotting?"

"More like boy-catching!"

"Nice one!" Clawdeen, dressed in a hair-apparent minidress, slapped her a furry high five.

"Wait." Deuce took a step back. "What are you wearing?"

He scanned each of the girls, taking in Frankie's white hair streaks and green skin, Lala's fangs, Blue's fins, Clawdeen's exposed coat, and Cleo's mummified body. "Are you *crazy*?" he whisper-snapped, pushing them back toward the stinky fog machine.

Beyoncé's song "Single Ladies (Put a Ring on It)" began playing inside the gym. "They're playing my song!" Cleo announced. She held out her hands, and the girls latched on.

"Cleo, you're not single!" Deuce wedged his body between her and the door. "This whole Melody thing is a misunderstanding. I swear. I was just going to call you."

"If you liked it, then you should've put a ring on it," Cleo teased.

"Where?" Deuce lifted her bejeweled hand. "There's no room. The lot's full."

"Then park somewhere else." She waved him away, kicked open the gym door, and dragged the girls inside.

"Don't do this!" he called.

But it was too late. Beyoncé's fast-clapping beat lured the girls with the hypnotic power of a Siren's song, straight to the dance floor. Protected by their sisterhood and propelled by her dedication to change, Frankie moved through the crowd with superstar confidence.

Heads turned as they passed. Compliments landed at their feet like roses. The Glitterati would have been proud. So would Viv and Vik.

As they approached the edge of the dance floor, Bekka and her mousy sidekick appeared. *Without Brett!* It was a great sign. She stepped out in front of Frankie, forcing her to release Lala's icy hand.

"And who are you?" Bekka asked, obviously put out by the copycat costume.

Frankie considered revealing her true identity but quickly thought better of it. "I'm the Bride of Frankenstein," she answered innocently.

Bekka pointed at Frankie's bare feet. "Couldn't afford shoes after you went dress shopping at the dollar store?"

"Actually, did you know that the real Bride of Frankenstein didn't wear shoes at her wedding?"

"Did you know that the real Bride of Frankenstein had a *groom?*"

"I did," Frankie said smugly. "In fact, he was—" She stopped herself again. It was one thing to play with fire. It was another to roll around in it. "You know, you look good green," she said truthfully.

"You don't," Bekka countered. "Which is surprising, because green is your color." Her little friend stood by her side, texting.

"Um, okay, but that makes no sense." Frankie rolled her eyes.

The texter looked up from her screen. "Green is the color of jealousy."

"And you're obviously jealous of me and Brett." Bekka put her hands on her hips and then quickly scanned the gym.

"Why would I be jealous of *her*?" Frankie pointed at the texter.

"I'm not Brett," the girl insisted.

Frankie giggled, then waved good-bye. She was much too amped to take any of this personally, especially coming from a wannabe with wilted Marge Simpson hair and poorly placed streaks.

"That was hilarious," a boy whispered in her ear.

Frankie turned around. A black rose was floating in the air in front of her face.

"Here." The rose moved closer. "I swiped it off some Scary Fairy girl. It's for you."

"Billy?" Frankie giggled.

"Yeah," said the invisible boy. "I think what you're doing is really brave."

He slid the rose behind her ear. "Don't worry—I took off the thorns."

"Thank you." Frankie touched the flower gently, the way his gift had touched her.

"Awoooooooooooo!" Clawdeen howled from the middle of the dance floor.

"Awoooooooooooo!" everyone howled back.

Frankie squeezed through the sweaty crowd, anxious to join her friends. On her way, hands reached out and touched her skin.

"Awesome!"

"That green makeup looks so real."

"Killer costume!"

"Are those neck piercings?"

"I want some."

"I know, me too."

"She's got better seams than my baseball."

Frankie was thrilled but not at all surprised by everyone's positive reactions. She knew they would feel this way. There was never any doubt. It was all about proving it. And her friends, dressed as themselves and dancing with normies, did just that. Frankie peeked at her phone to note the exact time history was made. It was 8:13 PM.

"Yayyyyyy!" Frankie shouted as she joined the girls.

"Frankieeeeee!" they shouted back.

"This is a ripper, mate," Blue announced, dumping a bottle of water over her head. Her scaly skin glistened with a silver opalescence.

"Woooooooooo!" The normies cheered for what they assumed was reckless abandon.

Clawdeen's fur was starting to curl with moisture. Cleo was crunking with a normie boy who was wearing her snake crown. And Lala was all smiles and fangs.

"Look." She pointed at her pale forehead. "Perspiration!"

"You're not cold?" Frankie beamed.

"I'm not cold!" Lala whipped her cashmere cape into the crowd.

Their combined elation was a rush Frankie had never known.

"Hey, beautiful bride," a boy whispered in her ear.

"Billy?"

He turned her to face him. "Um, it's Brett, actually. But I prefer Frankendaddy."

VOL-TAGE!

Gripping her lace-covered shoulders, thumb-rubbing her skin, he stood before her in a dark suit. Mint-green skin, bolts, seams, and forward-combed bangs: He was the complete package. And he had come for her.

In her fantasy, they were hidden under the stairwell. And yet there they stood, in the middle of the party. Surrounded by normies and RADs. Openly touching. Looking into each other's eyes. Not afraid.

He ran his hand over her streaked black hair. It tingled with electricity.

"I'm glad you decided to wear it down instead of in that big bouffie thing." He smiled with his denim-blue eyes. "It's much hotter."

Frankie couldn't reply. She couldn't do anything but stare.

Is this how zombies feel?

With warm hands, he held her neck...pulled her face toward his...and first-kissed her. The way people kiss on soap operas. Only better.

Much better.

Frankie began to spark. Then she drifted off like a helium balloon liberated from a birthday bouquet. As her body floated higher, the world below got smaller and smaller. Sounds lost their meaning. Responsibilities were pointless. Consequences became unfathomable. Her entire existence was about this very moment. Nothing before. Nothing after.

Just *now*.

He thumb-rubbed her neck seams with increasing pressure, as their kiss intensified. Frankie floated higher. Pleased with herself for having washed and oiled her seams. Proud of how soft and malleable they must feel to him. Certain they would end up being one of the things he loved most about her.

He gripped her head. Moved it from side to side. As if leading them in a dance that he choreographed just for them. *Hmmmm.* She liked that idea. A dance just for—

SKRRRRITCH!

A sudden sharp pain sliced through Frankie's neck. Her lips flash froze. Sparks flared in front of her eyes. Dizziness and disorientation overcame her. She was a teddy bear in a washing machine. Then it stopped. All she saw was black suit fabric. And all she heard was "Aaaaaaaaaaaaaaaaaaaaaaaaaaaaaaaaaaaaaaaaaa aaaaaaaaaaaaaaaaaaaaaahhh!"

Her head launched skyward with rocket force. She was face-to-face with Brett. His denim-blue eyes were fading. They rolled left. Right. Then back. His lids shut. He began to wobble. Frankie wobbled too. They were falling…falling…

They crashed onto the gym floor. Her body, limp as a rag doll, landed on his. Her head rolled toward the DJ booth.

"Eeeeeeeeeeeeeeeeeeeeek!"

Screams, frantic footsteps, and widespread panic blended into a noisy, chaotic stew. A giant boot pulled back as if gearing up to kick her, but a gust of wind with hands swooped her up and carried her away.

"That head is floating!"

"It's FLOATING!"

"FLOATING!"

"FLOATING HEAD!"

Nothing was clear. Fractured images shook all around her like vibrating puzzle pieces.

"MONSTER!" someone shouted. It might have been Bekka, but it was impossible to tell for sure.

"Floating monster head!" someone yelled.

"Grab her body," a boy whispered. "Don't let anyone see it. I'll meet you by Claude's car."

"Billy? Is that you?" Frankie tried to ask. But the head jostling and searing neck pain made it impossible to speak.

Reeeeewooooo reeeeewooooo reeeeewoooooo...

The monster alarm sounded.

"Everyone on the tables!"

Reeeeewooooo reeeeewooooo reeeeewoooooo...

"Grab chairs!"

"Up! Up!"

"Hurry!"

Reeeeewooooo reeeeewooooo reeeeewoooooo...

"Now scream!"

"Arggggrgggrgggrgggrgggr!"

"Louder!"

A cloud of stinky fog enveloped Frankie. She squeezed her eyes shut, no longer able to endure the pain. Falling into darkness, she wondered what her world would be like the next time she opened her eyes.

Reeeeewooooo reeeeewooooo reeeeewoooooo...

Assuming that there would be a next time.

CHAPTER TWENTY-TWO
MONSTER HIGH

Melody and Jackson had been enjoying a post-dance cooldown in an unpopulated corner of the gym when the incident occurred. A swell of screams from the dance floor didn't distract her from Jackson's hilarious stories about their freaky neighbors, or the way he'd punctuate each one with a soft kiss. It wasn't until Bekka started screaming "Monster!" that Melody decided to investigate.

"What's going on?" she asked a passing bat.

"They were making out, and this girl's head fell off!" he yelled as he dashed toward the exit.

Jackson scratched his head. "Did he really just say that?"

Melody giggled at the insanity of it all. "It's probably just some special-effects trick put on by Weeks."

"I hope so." Jackson bit a fingernail.

"Are you scared?" Melody teased.

"A little," he admitted, checking over his shoulder. "But not of the girl."

Most of the students and teachers were standing on the table-tops, jabbing chairs into the air and grunting. Those brave enough to fight at ground level ripped at each other's costumes, hoping to uncover any remaining perpetrators.

"MONSTER!" Bekka screamed. "MONSTER! MONSTER! MONSTER!"

The closer she got to Bekka's screams, the more Melody over-heard. It turned out the boy in this tragedy was Brett, and the headless girl *wasn't* Bekka.

Tracking the chaos, Jackson's crackling hazel eyes moistened with panic. "Melody, I really should get out of here," he insisted, holding the mini-fan to his face. A student running for the door knocked the fan to the floor, and it skidded across the gym. Jackson tugged Melody's arm harder.

"I can't just leave Bekka," she said, leading him through the chaos toward her horror-stricken friend.

"Why? *She's* not in danger," he snapped.

"Brett just *cheated* on her!"

"Monster!" A spastic ghost slammed into Jackson, then took off.

Four armed police officers burst into the gym, followed by a team of paramedics with a stretcher.

"Lock up your boyfriends! They're infiltrating. They're trying to mate with our species!" Bekka shouted, kneeling beside Brett's fallen body. She plucked a black thread off his finger and exam-ined it closely.

"Come on!" Melody gave Jackson a final tug toward the dance floor.

Bekka stood up, her cheeks stained with tears, her hair cone at half-mast. "There you *are*! Did you see what happened? It was awful," she said, sobbing.

Melody wasn't sure if Bekka was referring to the beheading or the cheating, but she agreed, either way, that it was awful.

Haylee and Heath were giving their accounts to one of the officers while a paramedic waved smelling salts under Brett's nose.

He came to with a start.

"AAAAAAAAAAAAAAAAH!" he began to scream.

"He's in pain!" Bekka called. "Help him!"

They quickly gave him a shot of something that relaxed him into a blubbering baby.

"Are you okay?" Bekka knelt at his side. "You thought that girl was me, didn't you?"

Brett circled his limp wrist and then giggled.

"Brett! You thought it was me, *right*?"

He looked at her, then burst out laughing. "What happened to your hair?"

Bekka ignored his question in favor of her own. "She wasn't wearing mango lip gloss! Didn't that tip you off?"

"Hey, Bekka wearsmangolipgloss," he slurred. "D'you know Bek-ka? She'smygurrrrrrrrrl."

"I knew it, Officer," Bekka said.

"Actually, it's Sergeant Garrett."

"That wasn't a kiss, Sergeant Garrett. It was a brain suck. That's what they do! They lure guys in and then drain their brains. You have to find her. You have to stop her!" She handed him the tiny thread. "Send this to forensics. It's our only lead."

"I have my best officers going door-to-door right now," he

assured her, dropping the thread into a plastic baggie. "If there are any more nonhumans in this town, I'll find them. Just like my grandfather did back in his day."

Jackson tugged Melody's sleeve. "I should really go."

The paramedics lifted Brett onto the stretcher.

"Where are you taking him?" Bekka asked.

"Salem Hospital."

"I'm going with you," Bekka insisted.

"Are you family?" asked one of the paramedics.

"I'm his bride."

Jackson peeled off his sweater. His pillow hump fell to the floor. "It's getting *sweaty* in here! We should probably go."

"Melly," Bekka called, scooting to catch up to the stretcher. "Haylee's going to stick around and interview the witnesses. You head out and try and find that...*thing*. I'll check in from the hospital."

"You want me to *find* it?" Melody asked incredulously. "You don't actually think there's a real *thing* out there, do you? It was a trick."

"That was no trick," Bekka warned. "Once you find the monster, turn the information over to me, and I'll take care of it." She waved. "Be careful!"

"How am I supposed to find an imaginary monster?" Melody asked Jackson.

"I don't know, but I need to get outside." He pulled her arm.

"Melody, where are you going?" Haylee marched over and set down her basket of bugs.

Jackson tugged Melody's arm.

"I'm just going to get some air," she explained.

"There's no time!" Haylee snapped. "You need to seize the beast!" She smacked her own head. "Crap! Of all the times to leave my camera in Mr. Madden's car. I could have taken her picture so we could make posters." She turned around and urged the few remaining students to hand over their cameras—at least she could document the scene of the crime.

For such a petite girl, Haylee was quite a force.

"Melody, come on!" Jackson tugged her arm again. "If they find out what I am, they'll come after me."

"Why would they come after *you*? You're not a..." She paused, realizing she had no idea what he was. Did descending from Dr. Jekyll and Mr. Hyde really make him a *monster*?

Haylee stomped back over to them. "Get moving! Melody, you have to come through for Bekka. She would do it for you. Friends first, remember?"

Suddenly Melody felt like a Ping-Pong ball. Getting whacked from one side to the other with very little say in the matter. She wanted to be there for Jackson *and* for Bekka. But choosing one meant disappointing the other.

"I know, but—"

"Melody, let's go!" Jackson tugged, his forehead drenched in sweat.

"One second!"

"Do the right thing," Haylee advised before hurrying off to conduct her investigation.

"Come on!" Jackson demanded through clenched teeth.

Melody sighed. Confusion was swirling all around her. And now it was inside her too. The hand of regret smacked her across the face. Why had she left Beverly Hills? Why had she fixed her downward-facing camel nose? If she had still been Smellody, no one would be fighting for her. And she wouldn't be in this impossible situation.

Standing in the middle of an almost-empty gym, surrounded by torn costumes, smashed hors d'oeuvres, scattered chairs, and tables marred by boot prints, Melody froze like an overloaded hard drive.

Jackson released Melody's hand.

She turned to him but couldn't speak.

His glasses were off, and disappointment filled his eyes. "You *again?*" He untucked the white undershirt from his jeans. "Why do you keep popping up? No offense, but you're sooooo serious."

D.J. was back.

"Where's my Firecracker?" he shouted. "Fire-crackerrrr, where are youuuuuu?"

He lifted his palm to high-five Melody. "No offense, right? It's just that there's no music in this place, and I need something more...*lively.*"

"I understand." Melody high-fived him back and then waved good-bye. Instead of running after him, trying to protect him, or finding him a safe ride home, she watched him go. She *let* him go.

Melody took a puff of her inhaler and then charged through the fog by the school doors. She had no idea how she was getting home. No idea who to save first. Best friend or boyfriend? Wasn't that the eternal question?

Outside, squad cars flashed their lights while police officers urged kids to get home quickly and safely. The wind blew in strong, short gusts, like an asthmatic trying to deliver an urgent message. It rattled the red party cups that littered the emptying parking lot, creating the ideal score for a campy monster hunt—something Melody would have appreciated had she not felt like the biggest monster of them all.

"Need a ride?"

Melody turned to find Candace emerging from the fog-filled doorway. Dressed in a black lace minidress, black glitter wings, and a head full of black roses, she descended the steps with the grace of a Radio City Rockette.

The draining feeling of adrenaline going back to wherever it came from slackened Melody's entire body. Her limbs loosened, her heartbeat slowed, and her breathing stabilized. Her Scary Fairy godmother had arrived. "What are you still doing here?"

"I couldn't leave a scene like that without knowing you were okay," Candace said, like it should have been obvious. "Besides, that was the most fun I've had since we moved here. Much more wild than any Beverly Hills High dance, that's for sure."

Melody tried to laugh. "Let's just go."

"Look." Candace pointed at the white announcement board in front of the school. Someone had changed the black letters around, so instead of MERSTON HIGH, it now read MONSTER HIGH.

"Ha!" Melody said, without laughing.

On the short drive back to Radcliffe Way, Melody counted seven police cars whooshing by. The silent car stereo created a hush that was louder than any siren. Candace was the type to blast music even when her father asked her to move the car from the driveway to the road. She was doing what Glory did: smoking

Melody out of her cave with silence, counting on the fact that the noise in her brain would become so deafening that she'd need to spill some of it out. And where better than the tranquil space they were inhabiting? It was an empty bowl just waiting to be filled.

By the time they got to the top of their street, Melody started leaking. "Question."

"Yes," Candace expectantly, eyes fixed on the dark street ahead.

"Have you ever had to choose sides between a friend and a boyfriend?"

Candace nodded.

"Which side are you supposed to pick?"

"The right one."

"What if they're both right?"

"They're not."

"But they *are*," Melody insisted. "That's the problem."

"No." Candace rolled slowly past a police cruiser. "They both *think* they're right. But who do *you* think is right? Which side represents the thing you think is worth fighting for?"

Melody glanced out her window as though she was expecting the answer to be revealed on a neighbor's lawn. Every house except hers had its lights off. "I dunno."

"You do," Candace insisted. "You just don't have the courage to be honest with yourself. Because then you'd have to do the thing you don't want to do, and you hate doing anything that's hard. Which is why you gave up singing and why you have no life and why you've always been a—"

"Um, okay! Can we get back to the part where you were sounding like Oprah?"

"I'm just saying, Melly, what would you do if you weren't afraid? That's your answer. That's your side." She turned into the circular driveway and put the BMW SUV in PARK. "And if you don't choose it, you're lying to yourself and everyone around you." She opened the door and grabbed her purse. "Oprah out!"

The door slammed behind her.

Melody sat back, enjoying the last bit of heat before the car cooled. She forced herself to see both sides. Not from Bekka's or Jackson's perspective, but from her own. Loyalty versus acceptance. With every second that passed, a little more warmth left the car.

By the time Melody had reached her final decision, she was cold.

CHAPTER TWENTY-THREE
FREAK OUT

It smelled like life had stopped and all that remained were cold sterile instruments. Bright lights. Chemical solutions. Glass. Metal. Rubber surgical gloves. And something else Frankie couldn't quite place...She tried to open her eyes, but her lids seemed locked. Her limbs, shackled. Her voice, muted. They say dogs can smell fear, so it must have an odor. Maybe that was it, then. She was smelling fear.

Voices expressed it all around her. It spilled from their mouths like a sponge being squeezed.

"It's a witch hunt out there."

"I had two cops nosing around my attic for the last hour."

"Our lives are ruined."

"I don't understand. How can you not notice your own daughter sneaking out of the house?"

"You call that good parenting?"

"I call it a danger to society, especially *our* society."

"And what about the normie boy? If he doesn't recover, this will make national news."

"If it hasn't already."

"I assure you," Viveka said with a sniff, "we are devastated about this. And have just as much to lose as you do. Viktor and I will do everything we can to see that this never happens again."

"Never happens *again*? We have bigger problems. How do we deal with what is happening *now*? My Lala will need to have her fangs removed if this keeps up. Her *fangs*!"

"Clawdeen and her brothers will need laser hair removal. Their pride will be shot. And with winter coming...they'll freeze!"

"At least you know where your kids are. Jackson hasn't come home yet. Every time I hear a police siren, I have to breathe into a bag. What if they start rounding up suspects? What if they—" Ms. J burst into tears.

"Everyone, please." Viktor's tone was low and weary. "While we accept full responsibility for tonight's...mishap, keep in mind that we have more at stake than any of you." He sniffed, and then blew his nose. "This is *our* daughter they're looking for. Our *daughter*. And, yes, she did something irreparable, but she is the one being hunted. My baby. Not yours!"

"Not *yet*."

"They're looking for a green headless girl from a monster costume party," Viktor said. "We can say it was a prank."

"Some prank."

"Viveka and I will do whatever it takes to make this go away. And we're starting by pulling Frankie out of Merston. She's going to be home schooled and forbidden to leave the house."

"I think you should leave Salem."

"Yeah!"

"Agreed."

"Leave Salem?" Viktor boomed. "I thought this was a community! How dare you turn your backs on us after all we've—"

"I think we've all had a long night," Viveka jumped in. "How about we reconvene in the morning."

"But—"

"Good night," Viveka said.

The computer hummed a final note and then shut down.

"I can't believe this is happening!" Viveka wept. "We *can't* move. What about our jobs? Your research grant? Our home? Where will we go?"

Viktor sighed. "I have no idea." He taped the last piece of gauze to Frankie's stitches, and then he dimmed the lights. "The good news is we have nothing left to fear."

"Why?"

"Our worst nightmare just came true."

Frankie's Fab door clicked shut behind them.

Alone and semiconscious, she dipped in and out of sleep. But no matter what state she was in, she could not escape her overwhelming guilt for destroying so many people's lives. In her dreams, the guilt presented itself in many forms. She was causing deadly avalanches, steering sinking ships, terrifying orphans, pushing her parents off a cliff, and kissing Brett with deadly scissor-lips.

After each dream, Frankie woke with a start, soaked in tears. But she found no relief in the peaceful silence of her room, because there everything was real. And the guilt was too immense to bear. Each time she opened her eyes, she'd quickly shut them. And wish that she had woken for the very last time.

CHAPTER TWENTY-FOUR
BEK AND CALL

Melody's finger hovered over the doorbell. Pushing it meant more than possibly waking some people up. It meant she had chosen a side.

She pressed the button and stepped back. Her heart began to accelerate. She wasn't afraid of the door that was about to open. Rather, the one about to close.

"Who is it?"

"Melody Carver. I'm a friend of—"

"Come in," said Ms. J, wearing a black chenille robe and clutching a balled-up tissue in her hands. She peered over Melody's shoulder and then quickly locked the door with a chain. The back of her bob had been pulled into a squat ponytail, and mascara smudges marked her cheeks like Rorschach inkblots. Without her hard-edged Woody Allen glasses, she looked like a regular worried mom.

Melody peeked inside the dimly lit home. The dark funeral-parlor-style furniture seemed to sag more than Melody remembered. Like there was sadness in its dusty fibers. "Is Jackson home?"

She lifted the tissue to her lips and shook her head. "I was hoping you knew where he was. He should have been back already. And with everything that's...I'm just worried, that's all. It's complicated."

"I know."

Ms. J smiled in appreciation of Melody's sympathy.

"No." Melody touched the soft chenille sleeve of her robe. "I mean, I know about Jackson."

"Excuse me?" Her expression hardened.

"I know what happens to him when he sweats. I know what he becomes, and I know why."

Ms. J's hazel eyes became shifty. Like she couldn't decide whether to club Melody over the head with a fire poker or run. "How? How do you know?"

"He told me," she lied. "But don't worry." Melody took her hand. It was cold. "I won't tell a soul. I'm here to help. I'll find him."

"Melody, you don't understand what's at stake if word about Jackson gets out. It's more complicated than you know. More complicated than he knows. A lot of people could get hurt."

"You have my word." Melody raised her right palm, ready to commit. Not because she had a crush on him. Or because his kisses woke her insides like a bite of chocolate cheesecake. But because finding Jackson meant saving him from himself, and the "self" was Melody's greatest adversary as well. The boyfriend-stealing monster, however, was Bekka's fight. And if "friends first" was truly her credo, she'd understand.

Melody raced across the dark street to get her bike and a flashlight. Asking her parents or Candace for a ride would mean violating Ms. J's trust. And she couldn't do that. She *wouldn't* do that. Finding Jackson and bringing him home safely was going to be her first big accomplishment. And it would have nothing to do with symmetry, noses, or being related to Candace. This rescue mission would show Melody what she was made of. As opposed to what Beau could make of her.

"How was the dance?" Glory called from the living room. She lifted her teacup off the side table and walked into the kitchen.

"It was good," Melody said, following her. "Do we have a flashlight?"

Glory shook her head. "We're using lanterns now. They're in the garage in the plastic bin marked OUTDOOR LIGHTING. Candles should be in there too. Why?"

"I wanted to go for a little walk. The dance was stuffy, and it's so hot in here."

"Are you sure it's safe?" Glory rolled her aqua-blue eyes. "The monsters are loose." She placed her cup in the sink. "Can you believe it? It was all over the news." She snickered. "You gotta love small-town living. They don't know real monsters until they've visited our old neighborhood. Am I right?"

"Totally," Melody said anxiously. "Okay, good night. I won't be late."

Glory blew her daughter a kiss and then headed for her bedroom.

Melody hurried for the door. Eager to start her search, she pulled it open and bashed right into Bekka. "Oh my god, what are you doing here? Is everything okay? How's Brett?"

Did she sound as guilty as she felt?

"He's stable. But he had a hysterical breakdown and can't speak."

Melody pulled Bekka in for a hug. Bekka allowed it, but she didn't hug back. "You must be so worried."

"I am," Bekka said. "So, um, why aren't you out looking for the monster?"

"I was actually just on my way out," she said, proud of her non-lie.

"Good," Bekka said, without the slightest sign of relief. "Here." She handed Melody her khaki backpack. "You left this in my dad's car."

"Oh, thanks. You didn't have to bring it by tonight." Melody cringed at the unnatural high pitch of her guilt-laced voice.

"You know my rule." Bekka smirked. "Friends first."

"Yup, friends first," Melody repeated.

"Friends first." Bekka smirked again.

Something had changed. It was more than the shock of seeing her boyfriend allegedly kiss a monster. More than Melody's guilt for not chasing a special effect. The different thing wasn't in the air. It was behind Bekka's green eyes.

"You also left this in the car." Bekka handed Melody her iPhone. But when Melody reached for it, Bekka pulled it back and double-tapped the screen. "Look what I stumbled upon."

The video of Jackson turning into D.J. Hyde began to play.

"D.J.... D.J. Hyde. As in Dr. Jekyll and Mr. Hyde. Just like my

great-grandfather...who was super-freaky, by the way. I found some papers in our attic, and it looks like he did all these weird experiments with tonics back in the day—experiments on him-self! After he drank these potions, he turned into quite a wild man. I'm not into drinking, but I do like a good dance party.... Got any music?"

Melody's stomach lurched. Her mouth went dry. Her breathing was labored.

"You *snooped*?" she managed. It was all she could think of to say.

"No, Haylee did. She questioned your loyalty."

Why didn't I think to erase that? Melody could feel her heart beat in her brain as she thought of how Bekka's discovery would affect Jackson and his mother. Bekka was no longer the friend who tipped her off to Brett's scary pranks or brought her inhaler just in case. She was the enemy with a monstrous upper hand.

"Give it back," Melody insisted.

"As soon as I e-mail the video to myself." Bekka tapped the screen and waited for the confirmation.

Boop.

"Here you go." She smacked the iPhone down in Melody's icy palm.

"That video was a joke," Melody tried. "We were making a movie. Like Brett's!"

"Lies!" Bekka snapped her fingers. Haylee appeared from the side of the porch. The dutiful helper opened her green attaché and pulled out Melody's signed contract. The one that said she would never flirt with Brett Redding, hook up with Brett Redding, or fail to pummel any girl who *does* hook up with Brett Redding. She tore it to confetti and then scattered it all over the DID YOU REMEMBER TO WIPE? doormat.

It hurt much more than Melody had ever expected it would. In spite of all their quirks, she really liked Bekka and Haylee. They were her first real friends.

"Bekka, I am so—"

Haylee presented another document.

"Silence, monster sympathizer," she snapped. "You obviously hang with that crowd, so you obviously know where she is."

"Bekka, I don't, I swear," Melody pleaded. "I don't even believe this monster girl is real."

"I know what I saw." Bekka took the document from Haylee and handed it to Melody. "You have forty-eight hours to find her. Failure to do so will lead to a video leak of Paris Hilton proportions."

Haylee handed her the silver-and-red ballpoint.

"I'm not signing this." Melody stepped back.

"Then I'll leak it now. It's your choice."

Melody grabbed the pen and scribbled her name at the bottom.

"Date it," Haylee insisted.

This time, Melody pressed so hard she punctured the page.

Haylee pulled a yellow egg timer from her case and turned the dial all the way to one hour.

Tick-tick-tick-tick-tick...

"Forty-seven more turns and we're coming for you," Bekka said.

Haylee lifted her case, and the girls stomped down the steps toward Mr. Madden's Cadillac.

Tick-tick-tick-tick-tick . . .

They pulled away, leaving Melody with an unobstructed view of Jackson's cottage. The cheery facade looked back at her with the warmth of a trusting puppy—a puppy she was about to put to sleep.

CHAPTER TWENTY-FIVE
SHOCK IT TO ME

Frankie had taken the stand. She had been sworn in. It was time to testify.

So what if it was sweltering hot? So what if her makeup was melting and her green skin was exposed? So what if her seams were achingly tight? None of that mattered. Clearing her name in front of the RADs and the normies who were packed inside the courtroom was all that mattered.

She would apologize to her parents for betraying their trust. For putting them in bad standing with the RADs and for not heeding their warnings. She would tell Lala, Blue, Clawdine, and Cleo how much their friendship meant to her and that she never intended to put them in jeopardy. She would tell Ms. J how much she appreciated her guidance. Apologies would go to Brett for losing her head and to Bekka for making out with her boyfriend. She would thank Billy for rescuing her and Claude for driving her home. She would tell them she didn't deserve a second chance. But if they gave her one, she would never let them down again.

Then she would make one final appeal to the normies, begging them to stop fearing RADs; to let her father share his brilliance openly with the world; to appreciate her friends' unique fashion flair and hair growth; to allow them to come out of the casket and live freely...

But when the time came to speak, no words came out. She gnashed her teeth, sparked, and moaned like a zombie. Each attempt to explain herself became louder and louder. Women and children began wailing. Men jumped up on the benches and began stomping their feet to scare her away. But it didn't work. Mounting frustration made her moan louder, gnash harder, and spark brighter.

Finally an angry mob rushed the stand and began tearing her limb from limb. Green body parts were being tossed like salad. The pain was so unbearable, she let out a glass-shattering wail and...

"Ughhhhhhhhhhhhhhhhhhhhhhhhhhhhhhhhhhhhhhhhhhhhhh-hhhhhhhhhh!"

"Wake up! Wake up!" Someone shook her.

"Ughhhhhhhhhhhhhhhhhhhhhhhhhhhhhhhhhhhhhhhhhhhhhh-hhhhhhhhhh!"

"It's okay, it's just a dream, wake up!"

Frankie blinked and slowly opened her eyes. The room was dark and still. "How much?" she managed despite her dry throat.

"How much what?" asked a boy.

"How much...was a dream?" She lowered her eyes. *Ew, am I really wearing a hospital gown?*

"All of it."

Frankie shot up, ignoring the dizzying rush. "It *was*?"

"Yeah, Firecracker," he whispered tenderly. "It *was*."

"*D.J.?*" Frankie wiped the sweat from her forehead. It was hot under those electromagnetic blankets. "Are any of my friends here? How long have I been sleeping?" She searched the room for clues. Nothing was as she remembered. Her lounge was gone. The makeup brushes and lip glosses had been removed from the beakers. And the Glitterati had been stripped of their glitter. "Where's all my stuff? What are you doing here?"

"Whoa, one thing at a time," he said. "First, you've been sleeping for nine hours. Second, your friends are not here. They aren't allowed out of their houses. Maybe they called, but your dad confiscated your phone. Third, your parents boxed up your stuff because—and these are their words, not mine—they have been spoiling you for too long and all that's about to change. And fourth, I scored a ride with Billy and Claude after that lame dance. When they dropped you off, I kind of stayed and hid and—"

"Wait! The dance *happened*?" Frankie's eyes filled with tears. "I thought you said it was all a dream."

"Not that part." He chuckled. "Man, when those guys told me what you did to that normie, I almost peed my Jockeys." He ran a hand through his floppy bangs. They were damp with sweat.

"Ugh!" Frankie lay back down. Instinctively she reached for her neck seams, but they were under a thick layer of gauze. "What am I going to do?"

"About what?" D.J. stroked her hair. She sparked a little. He snickered with delight.

"About *what*?" she sat up. "About ruining everyone's life!"

D.J. met her glare with smiling hazel eyes. "You didn't ruin lives. You jump-started them."

"Yeah, right."

"It's true!" D.J. tapped the screen of his iPhone. "You're the only one with any spark around here." The song "Use Somebody" by Kings of Leon began playing. Like a dog with its head out the car window on a sunny day, D.J. closed his eyes during the sweeping guitar opening, and warmed up with a little air guitar. Once the lyrics began, he took Frankie's hand and helped her off the table. Then he pulled her toward him, pressed his cheek against hers, and danced her around the sterile, unstylish, un-Fab room.

"I've been running around…"

She thought of Lala and wondered how serious her D.J. crush really was. "What are you doing?" She giggled nervously.

"Trying to make you forget about Brett," he whispered in her ear.

She sparked.

He smiled.

They swayed past the shelf of empty beakers. The glass tubes seemed lonely without Frankie's colorful products filling them with purpose. She had hurt them too.

"You know that I could use somebody, someone like you…"

"I'm such an idiot!" Frankie cried. "I thought, 'Oh, he's into monsters, so he'll definitely like me.'" She scoffed at her own ignorance. "I didn't know anything about him. I just wanted to be with someone who didn't want me to hide."

"You are now."

Frankie pulled away from his cheek and searched his eyes. "Why are you being so nice to me?"

"Because I like you, Firecracker. I like that you're not afraid to go for it."

"Go for *what*?" Frankie wiggled her hand free and stepped back. She wanted to see all of him.

"For the things you want."

Frankie touched the back of her hospital gown to make sure it was still fastened shut. "Yeah, well the things I want, I can't have."

"Like what?"

"Like freedom."

"You can if I help you." He took a small step toward her.

"Why do you want to help me?"

"Because you make me want to write songs." He touched her bolt. It zapped his finger. "How cute is that shock thing you do?"

She giggled. "Pretty cute."

"*Frankie?*" Viktor whisper-called from the hallway.

"Ye—"

D.J. quickly covered her mouth and turned off the music. "Pretend you're asleep. I'll hide."

Frankie hurried for her bed.

Her bedroom door creaked open. "You awake?"

She held perfectly still.

"It's a sauna in here," Viktor mumbled to himself. Seconds later a whoosh of air shot through the vents.

I love you, Daddy, Frankie thought, *even if you don't love me*.

They remained silent and still for the next five minutes, just to be safe. But the anticipation of seeing D.J. again made Frankie twitch. He was like a gift she hadn't opened yet. She wanted to learn more about him. Share her dreams for change. Hear his. Listen to his music. And spark.

"It's safe," she whispered into the darkness. "You can come out now."

Nothing.

"D.J., come out!" she tried again.

Still nothing.

Frankie slid off her bed and crept toward his hiding spot under the microscope table. "You can come out."

He emerged slowly, scratching his head in confusion.

"Where did you get those glasses?" Frankie giggled.

"LensCrafters," he mumbled groggily.

Did you accidentally sniff formaldehyde? Frankie offered her hand. "Need help?"

"Oh, man," he said once they were face-to-face. "You're that green monster girl from the dance, aren't you?"

Frankie gripped her stomach as if she'd just been punched. *"What?"*

"What am I doing here?" He looked around at the glistening surgical instruments. "Did I say anything I'm going to regret? Am I your prisoner or something?"

"Are you *serious*?" Frankie cried. This was the cruelest joke imaginable. "No, you're not my *prisoner*. Feel free to leave whenever you want." She pointed at the frosted window where her lounge used to be.

"Thanks." He hurried toward it.

"You're seriously *leaving*?" Frankie gasped, desperately wishing for five minutes ago. "I thought you liked me."

He stopped and turned. "Do you know a girl named Melody Carver?"

Frankie shook her head, even though she kind of did. "Is this some kind of cruel payback for tonight?"

"I'm sorry," he said, squeezing through the open window.

"Then don't go," she begged as the room began to flood with loneliness.

"I have to. I'm really sorry," he said. "Nice meeting you."

"*Stay*," Frankie begged as he took off running. "Stay," she tried again, even though it was too late.

He was gone.

CHAPTER TWENTY-SIX
A HOT MESS

Pacing across her porch, Melody thought of those windup dogs she'd seen on display on tables in the mall. They'd yap, walk, sit, turn, and walk some more. Then they would bash into the side rail and fall on their hind legs. With a mini hop they'd return to all fours, ready to yap, walk, sit, and turn all over again. Like her, they moved but never got anywhere.

Where was she supposed to go? Should she waste her time tracking a fictitious monster? Figure out how to get that video off Bekka's iPhone? Bribe Haylee? Confide in Candace? Search for Jackson? Move back to Beverly Hills? She was ready for action. She just didn't know which action to take.

Sneakers slapping on pavement caught her attention. A slim figure was running up the street toward her.

"Melody!" he called.

"Jackson?"

She raced for him, propelled by the strength of a thousand regrets.

"I'm so sorry!" She threw her arms around him, right there in the middle of Radcliffe Way. "I never should have let you leave without me. I was confused. I had to make a choice. And I chose you. I did. I mean, I have. But now..."

Melody released her grip. His hair smelled like sweat and ammonia. "Where have you *been*?"

"*Jackson!*" Ms. J ran from the cottage in her robe. "Thank heaven you're okay."

Melody peered down the dark street, no longer capable of facing Ms. J. In just forty-seven hours, her son would be exposed as a "monster," and it would be Melody's fault. So much for her word; it had a shorter shelf life than sashimi.

"Hey, Mom." Jackson hugged her. "I'm fine."

"Thank you!" She grabbed Melody's face between her hands and kissed her forehead. "Thank you for finding him."

Melody forced a smile and then lowered her eyes.

"Come inside." Ms. J tugged her son's arm. "Do you know how dangerous it is for you to be wandering around tonight?"

"Mom, I'm hanging out with Melody. I'm not wandering around."

"At least get out of the road," she said.

Jackson promised he would be home soon. Then he took Melody's hand and walked her home.

"When did you and my mother become such good friends?" he asked.

Melody responded with a distant smile. "Maybe you *should*, you know, go home," she said as they climbed the porch steps.

"Why?" Jackson knit his brows. "Who's the split personality here, me or you?"

"Huh?"

"What happened to 'I chose you' and 'I shouldn't have let you leave'?" He sat on the swing and began rocking playfully.

"Jackson." She gently pushed the back of the swing. "There's a lot going on that I can't tell you about and—"

"Oh, and it's worse than everything you know about me?"

He had a point.

The wind, still blowing in starts and stops, rustled the leaves and then drew them back into silence. It sounded as if they were trying to explain but didn't know how. Melody understood their frustration.

"Something really terrible happened, and it's my fault."

He stared across the street and sighed. "Deuce."

"No!" she snapped, slightly offended.

His shoulders relaxed.

"What is it, then?"

Melody swallowed a deep breath of courage but still couldn't speak. What if he left her? She'd have no one. But how could she not tell him? He'd find out in forty-seven hours anyway....

She sat beside him.

"Um, so you know that..." She swallowed more courage.

"What?"

"That video of you turning into...you-know-who?"

"Yeah."

"Well..." She took one more deep breath and then...

"Bekkafounditonmyphoneandisthreateningtogopublicwith-itunlessIfindthepretendgreenmonsterwhomadeoutwithBrett." She squeezed her eyes tight, as if bracing for a slap.

But Jackson didn't lift a finger. He didn't jump to his feet and begin pacing. He didn't grab his head with both hands and scream "Whyyyyy meeee?" at the starless sky. He just sat there. Rocking back and forth, quietly contemplating the predicament.

"Say something."

He turned to face her. "I know where she is."

Melody smacked his kneecap. "Come on, this is *serious*."

"I *am* serious," he insisted.

"So she's...*real?*"

"Very."

"How do you know her?"

"D.J. kind of led me there." He smirked. "I think he likes her."

"No!"

"Yes!"

"No."

"Yes."

"No. This can't be happening."

"Oh, it's happening." Jackson chuckled, because what else could he do?

Melody stood and began pacing. Was she still on her father's operating table having some kind of anesthesia dream?

"So, technically, you have a girlfriend?"

"I'm not sure if they've had the *talk* yet, but she seemed pretty into him."

"Okay." Melody cooled. "I guess this is good, right? You can take me there. I can find out her deal and then give her up to Bekka."

"No, you can't," Jackson said.

"Why not?"

"Because D.J. likes her. I can't do that to him...or me, or who-ever....He's kind of like my brother, I guess."

"What about what this is going to do to *you*? And your mom? And *us*?" Melody's voice quaked. "If Bekka shows this video to the police, they'll think you're a monster. They could arrest you... or make you leave Salem."

"I can't, Melly," he said softly. "She was sweet."

Jackson's willingness to martyr himself for this...*thing* made Melody like him even more. He had character. Heart. Conviction. He obviously valued romance and relationships. And he was a much better kisser than Scarbucks. Melody didn't have to date a Candace-number of guys to know that those qualities were hard to find. Which was why she intended to do everything possible to save him, even if one of those things was a tad amoral.

"I understand," she said, placing a hand on his shoulder. "We'll figure something else out."

He sighed, smiling. "Thanks."

"Hey," Melody said enthusiastically, "so I have another way we can get that video back. It's in my room. Wanna see?"

"Definitely." Jackson stood. He stuffed his hands in his pockets and followed Melody up the uneven wooden steps to her bedroom.

"Shhhhhh," she said with a finger to her lips. "Everyone's sleeping." She shut the door behind them.

"Now, where are my notes?" She poked around the boxes.

"Notes?" Jackson shuffled from one foot to the other uncomfortably.

"I know I hid them in here somewhere. I can't keep anything lying around with Candace on the loose. She's so nosy."

"Hey, do you mind if I plug in the fan?" Jackson asked, ducking under her loft bed.

"Why? Is the heat getting to you?"

"A little."

"I think it's in Candace's room."

"No, it's right here." He aimed the plug for the socket.

"Stop!" Melody leaped toward him and yanked it away. "I like it warm."

"It's not warm—it's stifling," he said, then studied her for a moment. Suddenly he gasped. "No. Forget it! You can't do this to me. It's wrong!" He reached for the cord, but Melody pulled it away.

His forehead was starting to bead.

"I'm trying to help you."

"This isn't the right way." He wiped his brow.

"It's the only way!"

Remembering the ThermaFoil, she pulled the lavender duvet off her bed and threw it over his head.

Just a few more seconds…

"Melody, stop!" He punched the blanket, but Melody hugged it in place.

"You'll thank me."

"You're going to suffocate me!"

"I'm going to save you!"

He stopped struggling.

"Jackson?"

He didn't make a sound.

"Jackson?"

Silence.

"Jackson? Oh my god, please don't be dead!" She whipped off the blanket.

His glasses were off. His hair was wet. His cheeks were flushed.

"You *again*?" he asked.

"Hey, D.J.," Melody said, beaming. "Wanna go see Firecracker?"

CHAPTER TWENTY-SEVEN
CHARGED UP

A pebble bounced off the frosted-glass window.

Then another. *Plink.*

Frankie rolled onto her back.

And another. *Plink.*

She thought of a woman tapping impatiently on a countertop. Maybe it was that angry mob from her dreams, coming to put her out of her misery, once and for all.

She rolled onto her stomach, the lyrics of Alicia Keys's "Try Sleeping With a Broken Heart" playing on a constant loop in her head. Frankie wanted to stand on her metal bed and shout, "I'm trying to right now, and it's incredibly hard because I can't stop thinking about Brett, D.J., my friends, my family, and all the people who are afraid of me, so will you *please* keep it down?" But she didn't want to wake her parents. The sun would rise in an hour, and they'd be up shortly after that.

And then what?

Rolling onto her back, she wondered how much longer she

could avoid them by pretending to sleep. A day? A week? A decade? Whatever it took, she was up for it. Shame was an intolerable emotion. But it required the presence of another person to survive. Someone to *tisk-tisk* while shaking their head side to side, then to rattle off the ways she had disappointed them. Without that person, the emotion gets downgraded to guilt. And while guilt can also be horribly uncomfortable, it's an easier sentence to serve, because it's self-imposed. And can therefore be self-removed.

"Firecracker?"

Frankie sat up slowly, not sure whether she should trust her ears. After all, they were controlled by her brain, which had proven to be very unreliable.

"Firecracker! Open up!"

D.J. is back!

Frankie thought about playing hard to get and making him think she'd moved on. Girls did it in movies all the time. But she was under house arrest. Where would she be moving on to, exactly? The kitchen?

"Shhhh," she hissed, quickly covering the unsightly hospital gown with her black satin Harajuku Lovers robe.

Frankie unlatched the window. D.J. quickly squeezed inside, like a grown dog through a puppy door. The sight of him spread a neon rainbow across her stormy day. Which was odd, since she had been all about Brett less than ten hours earlier. Or maybe she was all about D.J. then too, but she just hadn't known it yet.

"What happened to you? Why did you take off like..." Frankie paused as a second body began to poke through the window. It had shiny dark hair, black clothes, and a perfect nose. And it landed with a thump.

"Shhhh," Frankie hissed again.

"Oh my god, it's *you*," Melody said, awestruck. "Your skin is really gree—"

"What is *she* doing here?" Frankie toggled between confusion and rage.

"I have no idea." D.J. twirled his index finger near his temple, crossed his eyes, and then whispered, "I think she's obsessed with me."

"Whoa!" Melody wandered farther into the room. "What is this place?" She pointed at the glass cage by Frankie's bed. "Ew, are those rats?"

"*Seriously*, why is she here?" Frankie snapped.

D.J. pressed his mouth against her ear. "She's everywhere lately. I'm considering a restraining order."

His warm breath against her neck made Frankie spark from both hands.

"Man, I missed that." D.J. pulled her in for a hug.

"What's with that table? And those copper wires? And that switch marked HIGH VOLTAGE?" Melody asked, slack-jawed. "What *is* this place?"

"Why were you acting so weird before?" Frankie asked D.J., and she pushed him away, desperate for answers. "Why did you just take off? Why—"

"What are you? Like, Frankenstein's daughter or something?" Melody laughed.

"Granddaughter, if you must know," Frankie snapped. "And if

you keep interrupting me, I'm going to shock you like I did that day in the cafeteria."

Melody hurried toward her. "But you looked so..."

Frankie put her hands on her hips and glared. "White?"

Melody nodded.

Frankie sniffed. "Yeah, well, people around here aren't as go-green as they claim."

"I think you're awesome-looking." Melody stepped closer and reached for Frankie's hand. "Can I?"

Frankie shrugged like she didn't care. "If you want."

"Are you going to shock me again?" Melody teased.

"Maybe."

Melody studied Frankie's expression with serious gray eyes, as if it might reveal her true intentions. But whether it did or not, Melody still touched her. She wasn't afraid to run a finger along Frankie's wrist seam. Or maybe she was, but she did it anyway. Frankie respected that.

"Wanna touch my skin?" Melody asked, like she was a monster too.

Frankie nodded. "Feels like mine, only colder."

"Yeah." Melody rolled her eyes. "I'm always cold."

"Really? I'm always hot. I guess it's from getting charged and stuff."

"So, wait." Melody cocked her head. "You really get charged? How does that work?"

"Um, *hello*." D.J. pointed at his face. "Handsome guy in the room!"

Melody giggled. Frankie wasn't quite there yet.

Outside, the creeping morning light began brightening the

milky frosting on the window. Still, it was impossible to see anything clearly. Frankie's view—a kaleidoscope of blurry shapes and shadows—was a warning. Visiting hours were almost over.

"So, what happened to you?" she asked D.J., getting back to business. "Why did you act like you didn't know me, and just take off?"

"Maybe I can explain." Melody waved awkwardly, a stranger all over again.

"Just like a stalker..." D.J. mumbled. "An explanation for everything."

Frankie searched for a place to sit, now that her lounge was gone. But she quickly gave up once Melody began.

As the rising sun continued to count down the minutes, the normie talked about her crush on Jackson Jekyll, his overheating issues, his mother, who was Ms. J the science teacher, his deranged ancestor, and how sweat plus deranged ancestor equaled D.J. Hyde.

Then she went on about Bekka, jealousy, Brett, the kiss, the head incident, the video of Jackson, the blackmail, needing to turn in Frankie, the forty-eight-hour deadline—which was now more like forty-six—and how she didn't know what to do.

"So, let me get this straight." D.J. beamed before Frankie could respond. "I'm hooking up with both of you?"

Melody sighed. "Technically."

"Yeah!" D.J. high-fived himself.

Frankie touched the back pocket of his jeans. There was a sizzle-pop sound and then a flash of light.

"Ouch!" he shouted, grabbing his butt.

"Shhhhhh." Frankie covered his mouth.

"That one hurt!" he mumbled through her hand.

"It was supposed to." Frankie stepped away. "In case you weren't listening, *none* of this is good news. None of it!"

"Fine." He walked away, fanning the back of his jeans.

"So you're going to turn me over to Bekka?" Frankie's voice trembled.

"Well." Melody sighed. "I was initially, I guess...but..." She sighed again. "I don't know what to do. I don't want to hurt you."

"Why not?" Frankie looked down. A teardrop landed on her robe and bled across the black satin. "Everyone else does."

Melody looked like she was considering this. "I guess I know how you feel."

"Wait..." Frankie lifted her eyes. "Are you a RAD?"

"What's a RAD?"

"It's the nonoffensive way of saying 'monster,'" Frankie explained. "It means Regular Attribute Dodger."

"I was, but I kind of stopped dodging." Melody grinned, as if bidding farewell to a fading memory. She pointed at her nose for some reason. "But sometimes I wish I hadn't."

"Why?" Frankie asked, unable to imagine why anyone would want to go through what she was going through now.

"Because when you're different-looking and people like you anyway, you know it's for all the right reasons. And not because they think you're a physical threat who might steal their boyfriend."

"Huh?" Frankie dried her cheeks with the sleeve of her robe.

"I'm saying I'm on your side." Melody smiled a worried but pretty smile. "I don't want to give in to intimidation. I want to fight. I want people to stop being so afraid of each other's differences. So people like Jackson...and you..."

"And me," D.J. added.

"...and D.J. can live normal lives."

"What are we supposed to do?" Frankie reached for her neck seams but hit gauze.

"First we have to get that video away from Bekka," Melody said.

"How? I'm not allowed to leave this room for, like, *ever*, so..." Saying it out loud made it real.

"I have no idea," Melody admitted. "But I do know we have to work together, we can't get caught, and we have two days to pull it off."

"Oh, voltage." Frankie sighed hopelessly.

Melody offered her right hand to Frankie. "Are you in?"

"I'm in," Frankie said, shaking it.

"This isn't going to be easy," Melody admitted.

"Yes, it is," D.J. said as he lovingly lifted two members of the Glitterati from their cage. He held up a rat in each hand as if weighing them, and then kissed them both. "The hard part is deciding who gets me when all of this is over."

Frankie sparked. But this time Melody didn't pull away. Neither did Frankie. Instead, they continued shaking hands, cementing their allegiance in the battle for tolerance and acceptance...

...and declaring war in their fight for love.

ACKNOWLEDGMENTS

Special thanks to Barry Waldo, Cindy Ledermann, and my editor Erin Stein (no relation to Frankie) for trusting me. You have been voltage!

I would have hit a monster low while writing *Monster High* had it not been for the following people: Kevin Harrison, Luke and Jess, Alex Kohner, Logan Claire, Jim Kiick, Hallie Jones, Jocy Orozco, Shalia Gottlieb, Ken Gottlieb, and JJ's Diet Coke & gum delivery.

—Lisi Out.

Don't miss the next book from

Coming Spring 2011!